KIFRI

KIFRI

THE DOG THAT CHOSE TO
LIVE WITH MAN

Nick Korolev

To order additional copies of this book, contact:
Xlibris Corporation
1-888-7-XLIBRIS
www.Xlibris.com
Orders@Xlibris.com

Contents

For Mom and Dad, who never lost faith
and to Cassey, a very special Basenji friend (1978-1995)

AUTHOR'S NOTE

It is now believed by anthropologists and cynologists that the dog was domesticated several times throughout history at several locations from various local wild canid populations. *KIFRI: THE DOG THAT CHOSE TO LIVE WITH MAN* was inspired by the earliest evidence of the alliance between man and dog found in prehistoric rock paintings at Tessili-n-Ajer in the Ahaggar Mountains of Algeria. These paintings are very similar to those made by the Kalahari Bushmen and were probably made by their ancestors before they migrated south.

At the time the paintings were made, about 20,000 years ago, North Africa was very different than it is today. In place of the Sahara there were lush veldts not unlike the Serengetti. It was a land teeming with wildlife of which several species have since gone extinct—giant baboons (Theropithecus), Aurochs cattle (Bos primigenius) and giant lions (Panthera) to name a few. It is in this different world that we will follow Mikolu, a Bushman boy, on his adventure that would change forever humankind's relationship with the dog.

The dog depicted in the rock painting is the ancestor of the modern day Basenji Hound, the only natural breed of dog recognized by the AKC. The Basenji is what cynologists classify as a phariah dog. These small wild dogs are still found throughout Africa, the Middle East and Asia. They average 20 to 45 lbs in weight and all are of a spitz-type build with either rough or very short coats. Most exist in a semi-wild state living off human garbage dumps at the edge of civilization. The Basenji itself is still found in its purebred state among the Pygmies in the Ituri Forest and in several other locations in Africa. Basenji breeders world-wide continue to import the Basenji from Africa to strengthen their lines. It is a breed I have loved and worked with since my teen years.

In a way, I feel I have an ancient Bushman to thank for making it all possible. I hope dog lovers everywhere may catch a little of the wonder and magic from the story of that first time when long ago a dog chose to live with man.

CHAPTER 1

THE DOG AND THE DREAM

The Pleistocene sun baked the broad golden plains that rose to rolling foothills men would someday call the Ahaggar Mountains. The great Sahara had not been born. In the dancing heatwaves a small, dark shape moved with frantic energy as if searching back and forth.

The shape congealed into a nut brown boy with tightly curled hair. Around his slim waist was a zebra hide belt that held his tools of survival; a slingshot; hide bag of stones; a stone knife and in a net of woven hair, an ostrich egg shell that held precious water. He had seen ten rainy seasons come and go and his eyes now searched the parched ground for signs of the wounded gazelle of the Pranga clan the hunting party had lost. His name was Mikolu and he was desperate.

Before, in the confusing blur of rushing, tawny red bodies he had been the only one among the hunting party who had seen the direction the Bush Thing fled. He, in turn, ran after it before the rest of the hunters knew he was gone.

His urgency was the result of many pressing issues in his life that hung about him like biting flies. The most important issue was that this was the last hunt for large game before his Long Walk—a test of manhood that was quickly approaching. Right now he was regarded as a child and could only help the hunters by beating the bush to frighten Bush Things or by tracking wounded Bush Things.

It had been his uncle Mika's arrow that had wounded the Pranga buck and that was the reason for the rest of his desperation to find it. Mika was his mother's brother. When Mikolu's father died of a viper bite when Mikolu was but five rainy seasons old it was Mika who took his place. With love and patience Mika taught him the ways of the Bush Things, how to use a slingshot, and how to use the bow and arrow and spear he would be given upon his return from his Long Walk as a man. For him to fail in tracking now, Mikolu knew, he would deeply disappoint Mika. That would hurt for he loved Mika as much as he had his own father. What was worse, Mikolu feared he would lose what respect he had gained for himself among the other hunters.

Mikolu ran through a patch of tall, sun browned grass to a broad pan of sandy earth below a hill, his eyes search-

ing the ground. When he had lost the tracks on hard
ground they were headed this way. He stopped abruptly at
a small drop of blood on the bare earth by a set of hoof
prints. He touched the spot with his fingers. It was wet and
sticky. The wounded Pranga could not be far and was probably dead. He had to find it before other predators came
upon it. He started to run in the direction the hoof prints
pointed up the low hill. On his way, Mikolu looked at the
clumps of grass and thorn brush for the fallen Pranga.

A gurgling growl from the other side of the hill stopped
him in mid stride. Several short barks and more gurgling
growls told him the small dog Bush Things he knew as
B'sengi had the Pranga. If he hurried, he felt he could scare
them and get it away from them.

He knew them well from many observations while
hunting small game for his mother's cookpot. The dogs
of the B'sengi clan were not much larger than Owa, the
jackal. Their faces were foxy looking with a wrinkled brow,
their coats were short and brown, red or striped brindle
with splashes of white and tails that curled over their backs.
However, unlike Owa they were aggressive hunters that
lived in clans like his people and often hunted game many
times their size. As Mikolu reached the crest of the hill, he
slipped his hand into the hide bag of pebbles to select the
smallest ones to load his slingshot. They would sting
enough upon impact to drive the B'sengi clan from the
Pranga. He stopped short at the sight below. His mouth
dropped open and his heart fell.

At the bottom of the hill a pack of B'sengi he knew
lived in his clan's territory had surrounded a young male
Rowa.

Mikolu stood and stared as if his feet had grown roots.
The Rowa turned and trotted away from the B'sengi clan
to find a spot to eat his stolen prize in peace. The B'sengi
clan did not follow. They continued to yeowl, chortle and

bark in protest until the Rowa settled under the canopy of some low growing acacia saplings a bow shot's distance.

Mikolu's fascination with the B'sengis began to dull some of his remorse. He began to think and imagine. It was a trait that often caused him problems by distracting him from any task at hand to the point others called him a dreamer. Old Nendaka, the clan shaman, understood this more than anyone. Old Nendaka told him, "You are special because you can dream and see things that have not yet come to pass." Mikolu began to dream now as he watched the dogs.

They had lost the Pranga to Rowa, a bigger and stronger predator just as he had lost it to them. However, the B'sengi working together could bring down Pranga just as his clan's hunters working together could bring down the clan of giant cattle, Oom the Aurochs or the dangerous clan of Huma, the cape buffalo. If the clan of men with their skill and weapons and the clan of B'sengi with their keen noses, eyes and speed could become one, his clan would never loose wounded game again.

"Mikolu!" The voice of his best friend Turu shattered his thoughts.

Surprised, several of the B'sengi clan called sharply, "Wa-wa-wa!"

All the dogs were suddenly staring at him. Among them were some half grown pups. Then, they dashed off down the hill following the rare black dog that was their leader.

Mikolu turned away from the dogs to see Turu heading up the hill toward him followed at a distance by the other hunters. There were no children close to Mikolu's age in the clan. Even Turu was four rainy seasons older than he, sometimes seemed more like an older brother.

"We thought you were lost until we found your tracks with those of the Pranga," Turu said when he caught up.

Mikolu was glad to see him, but dread gripped him at the sight of the others closing fast with the troublesome Shonga rushing ahead. Shonga was eight rainy seasons older than him, much taller and well muscled. There was no love lost between them.

"I saw the Pranga head this way. No one followed it so I did," Mikolu said and smiled at Turu.

"The B'sengi took it?" Turu said looking at the retreating dogs.

"No. Rowa took it. Out there," Mikolu pointed at the big cat in the shade of the distant acacias busy devouring what should have been their meat.

Shonga reached them glaring. "Once again Mikolu the dreamer looses our meat."

"A Rowa took it, there," Turu said in Mikolu's defense.

Shonga looked at the ground and pointed at the tracks. "The B'sengi clan had it first. The Rowa took it from them. The Earth speaks the truth."

Mika joined them and scowled at Shonga. "Are you calling Mikolu a liar?"

Shonga stood up straight and tall making himself taller than Mika and gripped his bow tighter as the other hunters arrived. Waku, the wise clan chief, tall and handsome, and Katuka, the oldest hunter, were among them. Mikolu braced for trouble.

"He does not tell the full story. He is a dreamer too easily distracted," Shonga blustered. Then he unexpectedly turned on Mikolu. "You, dreamer. Become an apprentice to Old Nendaka, the shaman. He thinks you have a special gift for the clan. Maybe he will teach you to shapeshift into a Rowa. Then you can bring us Pranga and other meat."

Shonga's mocking words cut deep and embarrassed Mikolu in front of everyone. As much as they stung they did give a perfect opening for Mikolu to approach the other hunters with his new idea.

"I would not have lost the Pranga if I had a B'sengi to help me hunt," he blurted out.

The hunters all looked at him wide-eyed as if he had grown another head.

"A B'sengi among us?" Old Katuka said and slapped his bald head. "You might as well invite Rowa to sleep by our fires!"

"Impossible. The B'sengi would bite off your toes, Mikolu," Mika said, gently touching him on the shoulder and staring knowingly into his eyes.

"And worse. It would draw Kur into our camp. What a fool you must be to even think of it!" Shonga chided, shaking his finger at him and stepping closer.

Mikolu knew how dangerous the great spotted cat could be—more dangerous than the much larger Rowa. Kur feared nothing. Kur hunted by day or night often dropping from a tree onto its victim or exploding from the cover of tall grass that one would not think could hide a young Pranga. All had a particular taste for Owa, B'sengi, Oha the giant baboon and humans. The old, stealthy wise one that haunted the clan's territory had taken his sister, Tika, before he was born. It was still around. Only yesterday, the hunting party had found its easily recognizable tracks by a waterhole—one toe was missing on its right front paw. The thought of Kur sent a chill through Mikolu.

"Enough of this talk of B'sengi and Kur," Waku's voice broke into Mikolu's painful thoughts. "We have a meal to find as well as a night camp. We will begin the hunt again before the return of the day eye of T'chuka, the sky Rowa."

Mikolu noticed Waku had placed himself between him and Shonga to avert any violent outburst from Shonga. Mikolu could not understand why Shonga sought him out every time to bully. When he saw Old Nendaka again, he was determined to ask him and to also ask of the B'sengi clan as well. He would have pushed on about the subject with Mika, but Mika had closed his mind to it. With a sigh, Mikolu fell in behind the other hunters as they followed Waku away from the hill and the Rowa under the acacia.

That night, they ate a large S'sha, monitor lizard that Shonga had speared. The hunt for big game began in the morning. Mikolu ran ahead of the hunting party and made an effort to stay a distance from them, mainly to avoid Shonga.

The late afternoon sun found Mikolu alone upon a hill above golden plains. His eyes now searched the dry land below for game.

His world was ruled by the coming and going of the rains that coaxed the grasslands green and brought new lush growth to the trees and scrub which fed many clans of Bush Things as well as his clan. The dry season was still upon the land and game was scarce. The hot dry winds had turned especially angry on this day.

He watched a swirling cloud of red dust off to the left. He knew these swirling winds well from past seasons. They awakened destructive spirits. This one was quickly possessed by one such angry spirit and gained strength from the heat of the ground to become a giant cone-shaped column that stretched up to the sky. It swept along in a sudden, unexpected burst of speed across the golden plains.

He watched it lift a whole acacia tree right out of the earth. He knew the more powerful of these whirling spirit winds could carve a deep gully, where rain would gather and create a waterhole once the rains returned. Here, when the rains finally came, wild herbs, reed beds and creepers would sprout up over the years from seed dropped by birds. The new growth would flourish until another angry spirit wind would come and tear it all away again.

He knew it was but one indication that life itself was constantly changing in his world; that nothing could be considered permanent. The trees that stood for a hundred seasons were but temporary illusions. Trees were uprooted by wind or hungry elephants and replaced by young saplings from their own seeds.

As far as he could see on the plains all the way to the distant rolling hills was the territory of his people. He was looking for the B'sengi clan as well as game. His heart leaped when he spotted the pack running from the spirit wind. They were but tiny dots in the golden grass, but he watched them until he could no longer see them. No large Bush Things were in sight.

"Mikolu!" A voice sounded far behind him. It was Turu, running up the hill toward him. "Wait for the other hunters to catch up, Mikolu," Turu went on upon reaching him. "This is not a foot race. You will miss important signs if you run off like a young Pranga to the top of every hill."

Behind Turu three others came at a slower pace.

"But, from each hill I see Bush Things much further than just looking at the ground in front of me for tracks or broken and bent bits of grass," Mikolu said watching his uncle Mika reach the hill ahead of the others.

Mika had a frown on his face as his eyes met Mikolu's. Mikolu's heart fell when he noticed three fat T'woo of the guinea fowl clan tucked under Mika's belt. "Your mad rush up this hill let you miss tonight's dinner back in that acacia grove, Mikolu," Mika scolded. "You will not survive your Long Walk if you do not learn to use your ears as well as your eyes."

Old Katuka arrived next, frowned at him but remained silent. Right behind him was Shonga. Like yesterday, he looked upon Mikolu with distaste as if he were some slimy Bush Thing he found under a rock. He could feel Shonga's joy over his situation before Shonga voiced it.

"Perhaps the dust carried by the angry spirit wind has called Mikolu to the top of this hill fooling him into thinking it was the passing of a great herd," Shonga scolded.

Mikolu looked away from Shonga's sneer and mocking wide eyes and toward the whirling column of red dust. The B'sengi clan were in plain sight much closer now, searching the tall grass for smaller Bush Things fleeing the wind. Mikolu felt his ears burn with embarrassment. The B'sengi clan and his dream of befriending one of their kind would be the next target of Shonga's taunting.

"Ah-h-h, so it is not the dust. Look," Shonga said, pointing at the B'sengi clan.

Cringing inside, Mikolu turned away to follow Mika and Katuka down the hill with Turo beside him.

"It is the B'sengi Bush Things that have drawn his attention from hunting for meat again. Mikolu, you are a poor hunter. No woman will want you," Shonga scoffed behind him. A wife and child of two rainy seasons waited for him back at the main camp. "You could not track a Bush Thing if it ran through mud. Just as you failed to find that wounded Pranga yesterday before the Rowa got it, you again fail us in this hunt."

"Enough!" Mika snapped, turning savagely on Shonga. "It is time to join Waku and the others to search out a safe place to camp for the night. We will continue the hunt for large Bush Things with the first light."

They made camp next to a grove of acacia saplings. Mikolu was given the job of making the cook fire, a task that usually fell to women and children. It was a reminder of his lowly status among the hunters and Shonga stayed close watching to intimidate him. Mikolu let his mind wander far from his chore. As he squatted by the fire adding dry twig to a small flame coaxed from the friction of a stick and wood drill, he began thinking again of the B'sengi clan.

His dream of befriending one was now just beyond his reach. As he thought about it, he began to realize he wanted a friend as much as a hunting companion—a friend who would not care if he was too young or too old to play with or confide in: one who would never chastise him for losing game, but instead aid him in catching it.

Mika startled him out of his thoughts when he threw the three T'woo on the fire to singe off the feathers and cook.

"Dreaming about your Long Walk, Mikolu?" Mika asked.

He shrugged not wanting to tell the truth.

Mika smiled and patted his head. "You will do fine. Do not worry. Just remember to use your eyes and ears."

Soon the delicious smell of meat overpowered the acrid scent of singed feathers. It made Mikolu realize just how hungry he now was. A sudden overwhelming feeling of being watched made him look warily over his shoulder at the darkening land.

In the failing light, Mikolu saw movement near a patch of low growing thorn brush beyond the camp. He squinted at it. It paused. Mikolu saw a spotted hide. Kur! Instantly, he rose to his feet. Before words of alarm could spring from his mouth the spotted hide became the skin cape of one of the Kur clan draped around the shoulders of old Nendaka, the shaman.

The shaman appeared to melt out of the bush like a Spirit Thing. He paused and stood quietly leaning on his carved staff. A bag of medicine plants and charms to work magic hung over one of his thin shoulders. Around his neck was a necklace of Bush Thing teeth. An egg full of water hung in a net of woven hair from a belt of Kur hide into which he had tucked a stone knife. His hair was almost white and as bushy as Rowa's mane.

Nendaka fixed Mikolu's eyes with a stare of his own. As the shaman came closer, Mikolu saw a smile. It was then

that the others noticed his approach. All wore looks of surprise on their faces, though they knew Nendaka was out gathering medicinal plants at the same time they went out on
their hunt.

"Welcome to our fire, Nendaka. Stay and share our
food, " Waku said coming forward to greet him.

They shook hands.

"Thank you. I will join you. My journey has been a long
and tiring one," Nendaka said. He took the bag from his
shoulder and placed it and his staff on the ground near
Mikolu as Waku returned to his spot. Nendaka then sat
cross-legged on the ground by his bag.

Mikolu was always in awe of Nendaka. Though he knew
the old shaman was wise in the secrets of magic, he still
wondered how he could wander alone in the bush with
only an egg of water, his staff and knife. Though some
feared his powers of magic, Nendaka was special to Mikolu.
When Mikolu was still too small to hunt with Mika, of all
the men in the clan it was Nendaka who took extra time to
answer his many questions or gave council when his mind
was troubled. Each man had his own special wisdom,
Mikolu had learned. Yet, he found himself drawn more to
Nendaka's secret ways. Nendaka seemed to know his
thoughts.

"Something is bothering you, Mikolu," Nendaka said.

Mikolu looked from the cook fire to Nendaka.
"Shonga most of all," Mikolu said in a low voice so Shonga
would not hear.

Nendaka moved to sit closer to him. "Shonga is filled
with his own importance. We all know he fancies himself
chief some day. But, this will not come to pass. He is too in
love with power and this makes him try to get his way with
cruelty and intimidation. He will never understand that it
is not power over others, but power over self that is the
secret of true power."

Mikolu looked at him confused.

Nendaka patted him gently on the shoulder. "You will understand this some day. But, know this. Do not be concerned with Shonga. He has no real power over you unless you let him. As I have said before, it is you who will give the clan a great Gift. Perhaps he taunts you because he is jealous in his search for power over others."

"I don't care why he always makes fun of me in front of the others. I only want him to stop," Mikolu said, looking deep into Nendaka's dark eyes in the fire light as if the answer were hidden there.

Nendaka ran his hand over Mikolu's head in an affectionate way. "You must find the strength within yourself to stand up to him yourself and not let others speak for you."

Mikolu nodded, though he did not know how he could win against Shonga, who was so much bigger and stronger.

As the darkness crept across the land, Katuka pulled the meat from the fire with a stick. He divided it among the hunters and Nendaka. Mikolu took his portion to the edge of the fire light a short distance from the others to avoid Shonga's accusing glances. He knew that if it was up to Shonga his share of the fowl would be far smaller. When he took a first bite of the succulent meat, a movement in the grass only a few arm lengths away caught his eye.

He looked and found two eyes staring back, reflecting green in the fire light. Owa, he wondered, or T'hewah, the hyena. Again he found himself reaching for his slingshot and bag of stones. The Bush Thing came close to the edge of the fire light. It was a red B'sengi pup about six moons of age. It came a few steps closer made bold by the smell of food, its puppy curiosity and his stillness.

"B'sengi," he called out, and tossed a chunk of meat at her. He hoped she would take it and come closer so he

could show the others that the B'sengi clan would not bite off
his toes or attack anyone.

She dodged the meat, confused by the sound of his
voice. Then, she grabbed the meat. She dropped it and
sniffed it, suspicious. Mikolu figured she was not used to
cooked meat.

"Do not waste our meat on a Bush Thing," Mika
scolded.

"I will some day catch a B'sengi and teach it to hunt
with us." Mikolu said and saw the B'sengi pick up the meat
and bolt it down. Then she looked right at him as if she expected more and her boldness surprised him even more.

"This is what I think of a Bush Thing among us." Shonga
said savagely. He grabbed a stone and flung it at her, hitting her a glancing blow to the left shoulder. She yelped
and ran away into the dark grass beyond the light of the
fire.

"Shonga, you have no right!" Mikolu protested, balling
his hands into fists, feeling Nendaka's eyes on him.

"I am a man and you are a boy and until you return from
your Long Walk, if you return at all, that is all the right I
need, Mikolu," Shonga boomed.

Mika cast Mikolu a warning look. When he glanced at
Nendaka, the shaman held up his hand palm out indicat-
ing silence was the best for now. Mikolu wanted so to say
more. He was tired of Shonga's blustering pride and bul-
lying the others seemed to ignore. But, he kept his anger
in. Mika and Nendaka were right. Angry words would do
no good now. The dog was gone. A determination grew
and swallowed his anger. He would show them all. The
spirits of the Bush Things spoke to him, just like they spoke
to Nendaka. He was sure of it. Someday he would catch
and tame one of the B'sengi clan. It could very well be the
Gift to his people that Nendaka spoke about.

CHAPTER 2

THE LONG WALK

The night eye of T'chuka the sky Rowa was fully open and still low in the milky cobalt blue sky when his red day eye slid over the horizon. It was the height of the dry season and soon the day eye would bake the golden grasslands.

Long shadows of the thorny acacia trees that dotted the plains spread and mingled in abstract patterns of darkness and light. In the cool, dappled shade of early morning Pranga moved among a herd of Oom with wide spread white horns. Not far from the herds the smooth, bloated trunk of a huge ancient Baobab tree thrust up from the dry soil. Its twisted, root-like, nearly leafless branches seemed to claw at the sky as if asking for rain. A shadow within a shadow, Mikolu stood by the huge bole of the tree watching the herds.

The tree was sacred to his people. "Each baobab that comes up through the earth is but a branch of the Great Baobab that holds up the world," Nendaka, once told him. "It is the place where mankind began." And it was the place he was to begin his Long Walk to manhood now that he had reached his tenth dry season. It would be a test of survival in which he would use all the bush craft he had been taught for a Man never knew when the Gods would call on him to lead his people as a great chief or wise shaman.

Mikolu stood with only a wide hide thong belt about his narrow waist. From it hung his tools of survival; a stone knife, an ostrich egg shell that served to carry water, a hide slingshot, and a small hide bag that held choice stones of various sizes and extra hide thongs.

Smoke fragrant with the sweet sap of the Dakdak tree swirled around the great tree and seemed to rise with the haunting, wordless Going Away chant of Nendaka. Then the chanting stopped and the insects filled the silence with their songs. A rattle hissed. Nendaka's strong, resonant voice reached him.

"Mikolu is not a Man or a boy Oh Great Kongai, Lord of Bush Things and the Hunt," the shaman began. "His ghost now walks the Betweenn Time. No Man or Woman will see him. Now is the time of the Long Walk. Until the time when T'chuka's night eye is fully open again, he shall live among Your Bush Things and show You and the Unseen World that he has learned how to be a Man. May the Ancestor spirits keep him safe from Kur until he returns to this tree where Man was born."

The rattle hissed again. Mikolu stepped away from the massive trunk. Behind him, his clan was breaking up their camp to move on without him. Last night's Sending Away feast of Oom meat was only a memory. He was a non-person, a mere ghost now and his presence would not be acknowledged until his return. Though the pain of loneliness hurt him deep inside, he looked back at his people.

Mikolu spotted his mother, Shana. He recognized her at this distance by the shell decorated belt around her waist and white down feather of M'arabou, the stork, in her short, tightly curled hair. He watched her gather up a few wood bowls and her harvesting knife of stone and put them in a rough woven basket. Not far from her was Mika. Mika was talking to Waku. Both men avoided looking in his direction.

Then, Mikolu spotted Shonga, standing in the shadows and arguing with one of the older hunters. Turu came over and broke up the argument. Mikolu wondered what words had passed between them.

Then, the clan began to walk away in single file. The women carried their bundles and baskets of family possessions balanced on their heads or slung over their backs. The men walked ahead of them with their flint tipped spears, bows and hide quivers of arrows. The few young children ran about and the youngest was carried in a sling across her mother's breasts. Kur skin cloak over his narrow shoulders as the symbol of his rank and magical powers, Nendaka brought up the rear using his carved staff as a walking stick.

He remembered Nendaka's words before the Going Away ceremony. "You have a special power with the Bush Things that you have not yet discovered, Mikolu. Let them guide you on your Long Walk and always listen to your heart. Your path will be different from all the others who have gone before you. I will see you again. This I know as sure as T'chuka, the great sky Rowa comes each dawn."

As the clan drew away, Mikolu knew he was truly alone. Now he could look for help only to the knowledge passed on to him by Mika and prayers to Kongai.

Mikolu had appealed to Kongai for many things beforee, often leaving offerings of flowers, fruit or bits of meat stuck to thorns of young acacia trees. Sometimes the prayers were answered. Yet, Mikolu's biggest prayer had not, though Nendaka often told him some prayers take more time than others.

Mikolu left the shade of the Baobab tree for the open plains wishing he had a B'sengi with him. The sun was not yet directly over head and already the hard packed soil was warm beneath his bare feet. A vast living land spread out before him making him feel small and insignificant like Tik, the ant clan that crawled through the grass at his feet. Every shadow, branch and blade of grass held hidden eyes of Bush Things that watched his passage.

Mika had taught him their clan names; S'sha, the monitor lizard; Rowa, the giant lion; Oha, the near man-sized baboon; Ura, the great elephant; Oom, the Aurochs and many more. All were to be respected as brothers for they all danced in the Circle of Life and some were to be feared. The worst of all was Kur, the clan of leopards.

Mikolu had only his own thoughts now as his companions and they turned again to the story Mika had often told him of the death of his sister, Tika. Tika had gone with Shana, his mother, and several other women to dig roots. She was but three rainy seasons old and was the kind of child that had to explore everything. A brightly colored butterfly had caught her eye and she chased it past a thicket of thorn brush. The dappled shadows suddenly came alive. Kur rushed out and in one quick motion pulled down Tika and crushed the back of her skull between his powerful jaws. Thuna, Shana's closest friend, witnessed the attack and screamed, but nothing could save the child. Tika's Soul Journey to the Hidden World had already begun. Kur carried her body away before the first hunters answered the alarm. Her remains were found days later; a few bones, her crushed skull and the shells from the hide belt that was once about her tiny waist.

The thoughts angered as well as frightened Mikolu. The clan of Kur were the most dangerous Bush Things he must watch for on his Long Walk for they were the only Bush Things that would deliberately seek him out as a meal. The other predators preferred larger game or were easy to avoid. He could really see why shamans took the form of Kur for dark magic. He wondered if Kur, who had taken his sister, was really an evil shaman. And, if he was, why Nendaka never used his shape-shifting powers to become a Rowa and hunt down Kur.

Mikolu pushed the dark thoughts from his mind and paused to look behind him one last time at the Sacred Boabab. It was far behind him and heat waves made its dark form waver on the bright, sunlit plain. His clan was but a moving line of black dots beyond it. There was no going back. His childhood was dead. His life now lay in his own hands and wisdom. The final small part of his soul that protested his plight was quieted by the final reality of his situation. He wondered if others who returned from their Long Walk had felt the same in the beginning.

Mikolu turned away and walked on. He skirted the herd of grazing Oom. Some of the bulls on the perimeter of the herd lifted their heads and stared at him as he passed. One young bull full of his own importance lowered his massive head and shook his horns at Mikou as a warning not to come any closer.

Mikolu kept walking at his same deliberate pace. For him to run would be a mistake and only cause the young bull to chase him. Keeping part of his attention on the bull, he entered waist high grass and headed toward a grove of young acacia. A low, purring growl from the grass off to his right made him stop. Slowly, he turned, eyes searching the sun dried grass for the source.

His heart fluttered when he noticed the very tips of a Rowa's ears barely level with the breeze tossed seedheads. The cat raised its head slightly and Mikolu gazed into the baleful, golden eyes of a young female. He had been careless and let his thoughts cloud his vision, Mika's words to keep his ears and eyes open echoed in his panicked thoughts. Now if he was not quick, his inattention could cost him his life.

Ever so slowly he took a step backwards as he pulled his slingshot from his belt and loaded it with the largest stone his fingers could find in his belt pouch. As he took another step he prepared to let the stone fly. A quick glance behind him let him know no more Rowa were between him and the grove of young acacia. These trees were all climbable, but the trunk of the largest tree was not much bigger around than a man's thigh. Quickly, he turned his attention back to the Rowa.

She was sitting up and staring intently at him. Mikolu took another slow step towards the trees. Then another. The Rowa stood, then crouched to pounce. Mikolu let the stone fly. He was already running when he heard it strike her skull with a hollow thunk. She growled. He was halfway to the tree when he heard the tall grass hiss behind him as the Rowa passed through hot on his trail. He heard, too, the heavy thud of her big paws and it made him run faster than he ever thought he could.

He could feel her closing fast as he scrambled up the slightly inclined trunk of the largest acacia sapling to the first branch. Just as he hoisted himself to the second branch, he saw her rear up against the trunk. Snarling in frustration, she lashed out with one paw hooking the lowest branch and leaving deep claw marks. Mikolu scrambled up to a third branch and stopped. It was as high as he could safely go. The other branches were too thin to hold him. He sat down and hugged the tree with both arms and legs looking back down at the Rowa.

She was down on all fours circling the tree and staring back at him. She snarled and reared up again clawing at the tree with her front paws trying to reach him.

"Go away!" Mikolu shouted. "Rowa, go away! Please, Kongai, Lord of Bush Things send her away! I will never again let my mind wander. Send her away!"

Another Rowa roared in the distance. The young female dropped to her feet and answered. Mikolu looked out over the plains and found a mature male with a magnificent mane and two other adult females approaching at a brisk trot from the direction of the distant Oom herd.

"No! Please, Kongai, send them away!" His voice cracked. He was far easier prey than the Oom.

The three adults soon joined the young female looking up at him. The young female circled the tree again with the big male. Then the male reared up and tried to reach him with his paw and succeeded in ripping bark from the second highest branch. The tree swayed dangerously under the huge Rowa's great weight. He snarled in frustration and got down. He cuffed the young female out of the way and reared up again pushing hard against the trunk with his front paws. The tree swayed again. Mikolu tightened his grip and pressed the side of his face against the rough bark closing his eyes to block out the terror. There was the loud crack of wood splintering. The swaying stopped.

Mikolu looked down. The adult Rowas were all laying in the shade with only the young female still looking up at him. Sweat trickled down his back and into his eyes. It stung, but he dared not move to wipe it away. His breath

came in short pants and he felt his own heart beating wildly
against the trunk.

At the distant roaring of a Rowa all were suddenly alert
and staring in the direction of the herd. A huge dust cloud
hung in the air. Mikolu prayed that the Rowa clan had made
a kill.

The male below roared an answer that Mikolu felt deep
in his chest. All four Rowas were suddenly on their feet
and trotting toward the dust cloud and roaring. Their clan
was calling them away to a feast.

Mikolu did not leave the tree until the Rowas were
but tawny specks in the sea of golden grass. When his feet
touched the ground, his knees buckled and he had to hold
on to the trunk until he stopped shaking. He rubbed his
legs. When his strength returned, he drank some water
from his egg, then started out across the plains.

When the heat of T'chuka's day eye prickled his shoulders and the top of his head, Mikolu knew it was time to
find shade. The height of the day was upon him and would
soon steal his strength. Far from the Oom herd and the
feasting Rowa, he found a huge acacia tree, He circled it
at a distance searching the leafy canopy with his eyes to
make sure no Kur or Rowa were hidden up on its high,
thick branches. Then, he climbed it. He found shelter from
the sun and flies on a wide branch as high off the ground
as the head of Chia, the giraffe. Here he dozed away the
hottest part of the day, taking comfort in knowing that
somewhere beyond the Sacred Baobab his clan was doing
the same and probably thinking of him.

CHAPTER 3

THE PACK

Mikolu was awakened from his nap by the distant sound of pounding hooves and the hissing of small bodies through the tall grass. He opened his eyes to see a clan of Pranga fleeing toward his tree in great leaps and zig-zag dashes, the bright afternoon sun glaring off the horizontal white and black stripes on their sides.

Some ran past under his branch. He could smell their

fear. Curious, he squinted his eyes and looked out across the shimmering grasslands searching for the source of their panic.

A clan of B'sengi were on the hunt led by a black and white dog with a tightly curled tail. They had picked out their victim and were running it to exhaustion. The black dog, a red brindle and a tan brindle were on the heels of a buck with sharp, back-swept horns. They chased the buck in a great circle, then dropped to rest in the grass a bow shot from Mikolu's tree while four more of their clan leaped out of hiding to continue the circuitous chase. The first three dogs then walked slowly to a point where the second group was heading the buck.

Mikolu watched intently as the dogs worked the buck in an ever tighter circle to the black dog and his waiting companions. The buck's tongue hung out in an effort to gulp in more air. He no longer leaped and Mikolu knew the buck was tiring quickly.

As the three dogs took over the chase, Mikolu saw the black dog maneuver toward the buck's tail. The B'sengi grabbed it in his mouth as his group approached the waiting four. He pulled back and spread his legs hanging on with his teeth. His weight slowed the buck, but it tried a desperate last leap to escape. The second the buck tried to spring, a brindle dog bit him through the left hind leg above the hock to sever a hamstring, instantly crippling him. Held fast by the two dogs, the buck twisted sideways and tried to stab the brindle dog with his sharp horns, but stumbled. The B'sengis swarmed out of the grass. The last desperate struggles if the buck were hidden in the dust kicked up in the wild melee.

Mikolu, too, was hungry. He saw his chance to get some meat the easy way by chasing the dogs off their kill long enough for him to cut a portion. They would protest and might even threaten to fight, but they were small. He had often seen larger predators steal from them. He had seen Shonga steal

from them once several rainy seasons ago when they went
hunting together with friends. If he could put a big enough
scare into them with a noisy threat display as bold as any of
the Rowa clan, he knew he'd get some meat without getting
bitten in the attempt.

Mikolu climbed down from his tree and stalked slowly
toward the dogs as they busied themselves with opening
the belly of the carcass. He plucked the smallest pebbles
he had from the hide bag on his belt and loaded his
slingshot.

He decided to put on the best threat display he could.
Suddenly, he ran at the dogs, howling a war cry as he swung
the loaded slingshot in a circle over his head. All the dogs
bolted for cover in the tall grass except the black dog, a
brindle and a red dog with a chewed ear. The black dog
stood with his front paws on the side of the carcass, his
teeth barred, the hair down his back erect and a snarl rumbling in his throat. The other two backed away snarling
and showing their teeth. When the black dog hopped over
the carcass, Mikolu sent the pebbles flying.

Yelping, the black dog and his companions retreated
into the tall grass with the rest of the B'sengis. Mikolu kept
watching them while he quickly cut a chunk of meat from
the haunch of the Pranga with his stone knife. They watched
him just as intently in the grass with their necks stretched
so that their faces and ears appeared above it. The wrinkles
on their faces seemed to increase giving them a more quiz-
zical expression than ever. One even uttered a strange
yeowling call in protest. Another barked. When the black
dog made a rush at him, Mikolu quickly grabbed and tossed
a stone at him and he backed away.

As soon as he pulled the dripping red meat free, Mikolu
left the carcass walking away at a steady pace. To run away
would invite an attack. He kept looking over his shoulder to
check on the dogs. The black dog was the first back at the

carcass when Mikolu no longer seemed a threat. The others quickly followed and soon several snarling fights broke out over the choicest parts.

Mikolu smiled to himself over his cleverness. It would not take much to befriend one, he was sure. How he could catch one of the dogs, he had no idea yet. The young red one he had seen by the fire not so long ago was missing. Their dens were hard to find and the puppy season was long gone. He left a small chunk of meat on the thorn of an acacia tree and prayed, "Kongai, Great Lord of the hunt and Bush Things, grant that my people and the clan of the B'sengi become as one so none of us goes without success in our hunt for meat."

Then he headed back to the huge acacia in the lengthening shadows of dusk. He planned on making a cooking fire there and spending the night safe in the tree's branches far from the reach of the prowling night predators.

When he reached the tree, he dropped the meat at its foot and gathered up dry branches. Then, Mikolu dug a shallow fire pit with his stone knife and dropped in the wood. He started a fire by twirling a small, straight branch between his palms as he drilled it into another piece of wood under dried grass until it began smoking and flames appeared. When the fire was going to his satisfaction, Mikolu put the meat on a forked limb and stuck it in the fire to sear.

After his meal, Mikolu added enough wood to keep the fire burning through the night and then he climbed the tree. He settled into a crotch where two thick limbs three times the girth of his own body grew out from the main trunk. Here he lay in a half seated position with a good view of the plains through the branches and of his fire below.

Mikolu watched T'chuka's wide evening eye slide over the horizon into the dark expanse of stars. He had once asked Nendaka what the tiny lights were in the sky. "They are

the fires that light the way to the Hidden World," Nendaka
told him. "Other worlds inhabited by the gods float between
them." He had shown Mikolu a red point of light saying it was
Duat, the world of Kongai from where he sent the Bush
Things so long ago. Mikolu searched for Duat in the darkness. To spot it would be a good omen. He smiled when he
found it low on the horizon almost blocked from view by a
branch.

As he watched the red world of Kongai rising and listened to the night insects and the distant roars of Rowa,
his eyelids grew heavy. Soon, he began to doze.

Then it happened.

From a long way off a near human wailing came out of
the dark "O-o-o-o-o-o-o-o-w-w-a-a-a-a-o-o-o."

Mikolu was instantly awake.

"O-o-o-o-o-o-o-w-w-a-a-a-o-o," it came again.

The sound raised shivers up and down Mikolu's back
and arms. Was it a spirit that would raise from the earth in
a whirlwind to uproot his tree and carry him far from his
people? Was Kongai testing him?

"O-o-o-o-o-o-o-o-o-w-w-a-a-a-a-o-o-o," it came across the
plains again.

Mikolu was sure the source of the wailing was off to
his right, now. He prayed to Kongai that it would stay there.
It was too dark and dangerous to track alone in the night.
However, he was determined that with the safety the first
light of day would provide against most evil spirits, he would
set out to solve the mystery.

CHAPTER 4

KIFRI

Mikolu awakened to the first morning bird calls. Overhead the stars still blinked feebly as the midnight blue of night began to fade.

He listened again for the haunting night calls, but the spirit voice was silent. He yawned and stretched, then looked out at the world beyond the sheltering thorny branches of his tree. The first light of dawn stretched a yellow fire line along the horizon. T'chuka, the great sky lion was on his way to light the world with his golden eye.

Below Mikolu, the cook fire was but glowing embers. A bow shot from his tree a clan of Oha, giant baboons, were foraging in the grass for seeds, roots and small rodents. They were powerful Bush Things with sharp canine teeth as long as his middle finger. They could be dangerous, especially the big males who stood taller than he on their hind legs. The adult males were capable of killing Kur if they attacked the spotted cat as a group. When Mikolu counted them, he found their was one for each of his fingers and toes. He thought it best to stay in the tree and let them pass before he came down to search for the maker of the haunting night calls.

Silently and patiently he watched, hidden from their view. Five big males posted themselves on the perimeter of the clan while the females and young searched the grass and ground for food with their nimble hands. A few of the young still clung to their mother's backs while older youngsters played tag in the grass or brazenly harassed the dominant male.

Mikolu knew the chief Oha was becoming annoyed at having his tail pulled when he yawned, showing his sharp teeth in a mild threat. The youngster insisted on pulling the chief Oha's tail one more time. The huge male uttered a savage grunt, grabbed the youngster by a leg and flung him away. The youngster flew head over heels to land in the dust. The little Oha recovered and made a quick retreat toward Mikolu's tree.

The glowing embers of the fire instantly caught the youngster's attention. He sniffed at them. The ash made him sneeze. Then he reached out and picked one up only to let out an ear piercing shriek. He threw the ember down and ran on all fours to his friends stopping once to suck on his burned fingers.

Mikolu found it hard to stifle a laugh at the antics of the young trouble maker. The members of the Oha clan reminded him of some of his own people. Especially that one young one. The Oha soon moved on in their foraging.

Mikolu climbed down from his perch the moment the Oha were over the low rise to his left. He kicked dust over the embers to make sure they were out so no sparks would blow and start a grass fire. Then he set out across the grassland in the direction of the night calls.

All morning he walked through the tall grass and scrub thorn brush, the sun warm on his head and shoulders. He paused only once to drink the warm water in his egg. A distant, shimmering, unmoving, dark blob took shape ahead of him. As he drew closer to it he found himself in a forest of young acacia trees. The dark blob solidified into a low hill topped by a giant jumble of almost square boulders piled on top of each other. Surrounding the rock island in the sea of grass were old yellow-barked fever tree acacias that spread their thick branches over the rocks in many places. Such islands of rock were scattered all through the lands his people wandered. They were the stepping stones of the gods when the world was flooded, Nendaka had told him.

This particular rock island was unknown to him. It was a world of bright light and deep shadow where anything could lurk, spirits, Bush Things and especially Kur. Mikolu loaded his slingshot with a stone the size of a M'tuk, tortoise clan's egg. Cautiously he stalked into the shadows of the rocks not knowing what he would find, but well prepared to defend himself.

He slowly climbed a sloping boulder, scaring a few small N'gema, agama lizards, into scuttling frantically for cover in cracks. The boulder was not so steep a climb that he needed to use his hands, yet steep enough that he had to hunch over to keep his balance. At the summit he could see over the tops of the fever trees. One had an old deserted nest of broken branches in its crown.

Mikolu froze when he heard the faint sound of claws scratching on rock. Then something whined. Not a spirit or Kur, but B'sengi! He tucked his slingshot in his belt and ran across the tops of the boulders, leaping across the narrow gaps between them.

Mikolu stopped short where three huge boulders formed a pit as deep as he was tall and twice as wide. At the bottom was a B'sengi. Her dusty coat was a deep golden-red like that of M'Pranga, the impala, and her paws, tail tip and blaze on her face were white. She was the very same pup that he had fed by the fire. The mysteries of her absence from the B'sengi clan and the night calls were solved. She had bloodied her nails from her attempts at climbing out, but otherwise she seemed unhurt. As soon as her dark slightly slanted eyes met his, she growled and erected her back hair to seem larger and more fierce than she was. She was young, possibly no older than six cycles of T'chuka's night eye. From what Mikolu had observed in the past it was an age B'sengis spent exploring their world, learning the ways of the pack and beginning to hunt. It was also the time when strong bonds were made to the pack leaders. Mikolu smiled at his good fortune. That made it still the right time when he could befriend her. She needed a pack to survive as much as he needed a clan. Without the other dogs, she would easily bind herself to him once he gained her trust.

Mikolu laughed both out of joy and at her show of ferocity. It only made her growl louder.

"Quiet, little one," Mikolu said softly. " The Great Kongai has seen fit to bring us together. We must grow to trust one another if we are to become friends."

Nendaka had told him that every Bush Thing had a soul name by which one could gain an instant trust with them. The B'senji was far too upset to tell him hers so, he would have to name her. To do so would help in the magic of a friendship bond just as his name giving three days after his birth had made him a member of his parents clan.

He stared into her dark eyes for a hint at the right name. He saw a wildness there, a defiant and proud nature. She curled up her black lips and showed her teeth in a snarl. Mikolu ignored it for it was her fear speaking to him.

He wanted her as kifri, a friend, not a wild Bush Thing. That was it, he thought. "I will call you Kifri," he said gently to her. "Friend."

She stopped snarling and stared at him, cocking her head to one side at the sound of his quiet voice. The wrinkles on her brow seemed to multiply and she backed away until her rump touched the stone wall behind her.

"Kifri", Mikolu repeated and his dream seemed now within his grasp.

CHAPTER 5

THE FIRST DAY

Mikolu knew he would have to gain Kifri's confidence before he could ever lay a hand on her. The best way to put her at ease would be to share food and water with her, the two gifts of life. It was the most important step in what Mikolu knew would be a long journey. He knew, too, he would have to keep her in the pit until that special trust was attained.

To find game and water he would have to leave her to explore the rock island. He peeked over the edge of the pit one more time curious to see if her reaction would still be one of hostility.

Kifri looked up and growled at him. The noise started low in her chest hardly audible, then rattled up into her throat. It was still an intensely angry sound as if she were blaming him for the loss of her freedom and her clan.

"We will soon be friends," Mikolu said to her. "You will see. I go now to find us meat." He turned away from the pit and scrambled over the great boulders.

Quiet as a shadow, Mikolu stalked through the tall grass in the mottled shade of the yellow fever trees alert to the smallest sound in the brush. Such rock islands could harbor a large clan of Oha, Rowa, or the dreaded Kur. The shadow filled cracks in the huge rocks were a good hiding place for the many clans of S'shaa, the snake, the worst of which carried poison in their fangs. One such snake had killed his father. The thought brought a sad tug at his heart. All around the rock island the yellow-barked fever trees seemed to grow in a small forest, a sure sign that water was near.

He passed a fig tree and stared into its deep shadows. Nothing stirred but the vibrant green leaves in the light afternoon breeze. The light, airy song of a bird burst from the branches high over his head. Mikolu turned away to continue his exploring.

A bow shot from the fig tree Mikolu smelled wet earth. There had to be water near. He picked up his pace at the sound of a light scratching in dry dirt. It could be prey. He loaded a stone in his sling and slowed to creep forward in a half crouch.

A flock of T'woo, the guinea fowl clan, large, bare-headed birds with bony head crests and white speckled gray plumage burst from the tall grass in explosive flight directly ahead of him. Mikolu let the stone fly. One bird plummeted from the sky to hit the grass with a soft feathered thud. Smiling, Mikolu picked it up by a leg. He was not such a bad hunter after all and almost wished the bully, Shonga could have seen the bird fall. He shrugged off the notion and continued on his way to locate the water. He was sure he was close.

About half the way around the other side of the rock island the gurgling sound of running water reached him. Where the boulders formed a miniature canyon just about big enough for Ura, the elephant, to back into, Mikolu found a spring. A trickle of clear water poured from between moss covered rocks. It formed a pool deep enough for a man to swim in yet only wide enough for two of the Ura clan to stand head to tail. In the soft earth near it were the tracks of many Bush Things.

With great caution Mikolu stalked toward the water. Then he squatted and dipped his cupped hand in the cool water for a taste. It was clear and sweet, much better than the muddy water from the waterholes out on the plains. He pulled the grass plug from his egg and filled it with the sweet water.

Quite content with the gifts of life Kongai had bestowed on him this day, Mikolu left one of the T'woo wings on the thorns of an acacia sapling in thanksgiving. Then, he started back to Kifri by continuing his walk around the island to his starting point among the yellow fever trees. If he was going to share the water with Kifri, he would have to make something to put it in. He paused when he came upon a large fallen limb under one of the trees. It gave him an idea. Though the sun was low in the sky, he still had enough time to rough cut a small water bowl for Kifri. He could finish it in the safety of the light from his cook fire.

He put the fowl on the ground next to the limb and began hacking away at the tough bark with his stone knife.

He was sweating by the time he separated a chunk of wood from the limb deep enough to hold water. Darkness was swiftly approaching. He poked a leg of the T'woo through the hide belt about his waist to free his hands to gather smaller branches for fire wood and tied up a bundle of it with a thong. Then with the bowl in one hand and fire wood tucked under the crook of his arm, Mikolu walked through the fever tree woodland noticing his shadow made him look as tall as Chia, the giraffe. Already the cool night breeze rose bumps on is skin.

His load of firewood slowed him some and made the climb to the top of the boulders more difficult. As darkness took the sky from T'chuka's bright eye Mikolu got his cookfire started. Using his stone knife, he slit open the T'woo and pulled the entrails out putting them aside on the sun-warmed boulder. Then, he cut the T'woo in half above its hips. He threw the front half, feathers and all onto the fire for himself. The back half he stuffed with the organs and put aside for Kifri. Then he set about finishing the waterbowl, the smell of searing flesh and feathers wafting from his cookfire.

It did not take him long to carve a deep impression into the dry wood. As he ate his portion of the meat he smeared some of the fat on the roughly hewn bowl and put it in the fire a moment to harden and waterproof it. Then he notched the sides in four places and strung hide thongs around it so he could safely raise and lower it to Kifri in the pit.

He dared not try to climb down into the pit yet. Mikolu knew Kifri's fear of not being able to escape would drive her to bite.

As he tied the last knot and filled the bowl with water, he smiled. It was not as good a bowl as his mother could make, but it would serve his purpose. He tossed another branch on the fire and watched as the flames licked up higher to provide more light. Shadows danced eerily like spirit warriors. T'chuka's open night eye touched the tree tops with silver. Mikolu approached the edge of the pit, the meat in one hand and water bowl in the other.

"Kifri", he whispered.

In the shadows of the rock below he heard her stir. Firelight and T'chuka's light glowed on the rocks. It reached her and made her look like a spirit reflecting green in her eyes. She snarled at him.

Mikolu tossed the meat down to her. She instantly stopped snarling to sniff at it not taking her eyes from him. Then she gobbled up the organs snarling between bites. When he moved closer to the edge to lower the bowl of water, she left the meat and charged at him, her snarls turning to a screaming howl. She leaped at him snapping her bared teeth.

Taken off guard, Mikolu pulled back from the edge, spilling a little of the water on Kifri. Kifri slid back into the pit still growling defiantly and shook herself dry. She grabbed the meat and backed away to the far side.

While she busied herself with plucking the feathers from the meat with her teeth, Mikolu lowered the water bowl and tied the ends of the thongs to a heavy stone so he could pull it back up to refill. "See," he said. "I do not run. I am your friend. Here is water so that you will not die of thirst."

His answer was a growl from the moon shadows. As thirsty as she must be by now, she refused to go near the bowl while Mikolu watched her finish eating. He sighed and felt a heaviness in his soul. It could be that she would never accept him. Perhaps Mika,Shonga and the Elders were right. But, deep inside he felt he had to try. It took as much courage to try and fail, Nendaka had once told him, as it did to try and succeed.

"Kifri", he whispered. "Friend."

She growled from the moon shadows.

CHAPTER 6

ISLAND IN THE GRASS

Kur was there in the golden grass, moving as slow as a shadow. The burning green eyes stared so intense Mikolu thought they would melt him like hot fat in a fire. The whiskered muzzle and cruel teeth were dripping with blood. Closer and larger the spotted face grew until it was all Mikolu could see. The breath came out stinking of carrion.

Mikolu cried out in his sleep and sat up, his heart racing. Disoriented and frantic, he looked about him at the darkness beyond his comforting fire. The night calls of insects and the distant giggles of the T'heeah clan were mocking him. He shivered not so much from the night chill as the frightening dream. It had all been so real. He wished old Nendaka were with him to explain the meaning. It felt to him like a warning.

Thoughts of the story his mother had told him of the death of the sister he never knew surfaced like a ghost to prey on his sleepy mind. A deep sadness gripped him. Kur would never take anyone from him again, Mikolu promised himself.

His thoughts suddenly jumped to Kifri. He turned to look at the pit. Firelight just reached the rim. Quietly, he got up and crept close enough to just peek over the edge.

In the shadows below, he could barely pick her out in the darkness. She was curled in a tight ball with a paw placed protectively over her nose, sound asleep. He smiled gently to himself as he crept back to his fire. After adding another dried branch to the hungry flames, he curled up with his back to the warmth and once again fell asleep.

Bird songs awakened him. He opened his eyes to the milky gray first light along the horizon that announced the coming of T'chuka. Yawning, Mikolu sat up and stretched his arms and shoulders. Today he would spend hunting. But, first he had to check Kifri's water bowl. He reached over and picked up his egg, took out the grass stopper and drank a few swallows. Then he took it to the edge of the pit and knelt down.

Cautiously, Mikolu peeked over the edge. Kifri was awake and looked up at him. He watched the hair raise down the center of her back. A low growl rumbled in her throat.

"Do not behave so," he chided in a quiet voice. "I am your friend, Kifri. Soon, we will hunt together."

She went silent and cocked her head curiously at his words. However, the hair on her back remained up.

Mikolu took the long hide thong that was tied to her water bowl and hoisted it up. She came over, growling and reared up on her hind legs as if she wanted to follow the bowl out of the pit. Mikolu found all the water was gone. He poured most of what was left in his egg into the rough hewn bowl and replaced the grass plug. On his hunt he planned to stop by the spring to refill it.

"There, Kifri. Now you will not die of thirst while I am gone." He looked down into her slanted, brown eyes and she barred her teeth at him, snarling louder than before. He slowly lowered the water bowl to the bottom of the pit. Kifri backed away from it to snarl at him from the far side.

"Kifri." He sighed and shook his head wondering if she would ever accept him. He longed to hold her and stroke her silky coat remembering how his mother used to hold him when he was small and how much comfort he had found in her touch. Perhaps Kifri would grow calmer under the touch of a gentle hand. Now, however, was not the time to try it. Regretfully, Mikolu turned away from the pit and tied the water bottle thong to his hide belt.

He stood up and walked slowly across the cool rocks to the huge sloping boulder and climbed down to the tall grass. The scratchy grass brushing past his legs, he scanned the grove of acacias as he walked through it. No Pranga or Rhaha clan of zebra grazed here between the widely spaced trees and their absence brought him into an extreme state of alertness. His keen eyes wandered the shadowy, dark green, leafy canopies of the trees. He felt eyes upon him and it made him more uneasy with every beat of his heart. When he picked up the salt-sweet carrion scent of death, he loaded his slingshot with the biggest stone from the pouch on his belt. Then he spotted something in the lower branches of the last tree before the open plains.

He blinked once to clear his vision as T'chuka's eye edged over the horizon to spread its light and warmth over the land.

A furry arm dangled from the lowest thorny branch. His eyes followed it up higher. Mikolu could just make out what was left of a disemboweled Oha hung in the branches. Curious, he took two cautious steps closer. The discovery of what could be Kur's larder so close to his own camp made Mikolu realize he could not stay much longer. Given time, Kur would surely find him and Kifri.

A low snarl sounded from high in the tree. Mikolu's eyes immediately snapped up to the source and his heart beat so hard he feared it would burst.

Kur lay lounging heavy-bellied on a thick branch, gold coat on fire in the rising eye of T'chuka. To Mikolu it was as if Kur imagined that so long as he lay still he was unseen. The only thing that moved were the cat's yellow-green eyes as they focused on him. Where he found the gaze of Rowa merely baleful, that of Kur was malevolent and truly savage. He was sure now that Kur was different than others of his clan. Maybe he was possessed by an evil shaman. The big, spotted cat did not move, but his round ears were pressed back against his head at an angry angle. He was too full and sleepy to attack. This time Mikolu knew Kongai was smiling on him. He wished he had a bow and arrows to finish the war between Kur and his people. These were only the property of a man he would not get until his return.

Heart still hammering, Mikolu slowly backed away from the tree, ready any moment to let loose the stone in his slingshot. Not until he was a bowshot away did he dare turn his back on the tree and head at a swift walk toward the other side of the rocky island where the spring fed pool was located.

Mikolu's heart did not stop pounding until Kur's tree was out of sight behind the massive rocks. He then began to concentrate on searching for signs of game; trampled grass, droppings, a bent twig, or the scolding of a bird.

When the scent of moss dampened by spring water reached him, he knew he was nearing the pool. It was about then that he saw a flash of tan fur by a low growing thorn bush. He moved toward it silent as Kur himself.

Through the blades of the tall grass he spotted a Pranga fawn laying flat with its legs tucked up under it and neck stretched out. It was still young enough to have no odor. Any other of the great hunters of the plains would pass it without noticing it in its stillness, but not Mikolu. His uncle had taught him all the tricks of its kind. It was small enough to be easy prey. He knew he could catch it without a long chase.

Mikolu quickly fell upon it. The struggle was brief and he quickly killed it by grabbing its head and twisting it back to break its neck the way his uncle had shown him. It would provide enough meat for both himself and Kifri for two, maybe three cycles of the T'chuka's eye. He would not have to leave Kifri again except to fetch wood for the fire and drinking water. He prayed to Kongai that she would accept and trust him before the meat ran out for it was then that he felt he had to leave the island in the grass. He prayed that Kur would not find them in that time.

CHAPTER 7

ESCAPE

The sun was still high in the sky when Mikolu fin ished putting the last batch of branches down for the last small camp fire behind Kifri's pit. He had started several around the main cookfire to provide a barrier that he hoped would serve to keep Kur away. Fire was the only thing Kur truly feared. Satisfied with his handiwork, Mikolu transferred a burning branch from the cookfire to light the new pile of branches. Then, looking one last time at his ring of fires, he set about butchering the fawn carcass for the evening meal. He did not find this any more diffi-cult than butchering small game for his mother's cook pot and knew Mika would be proud of him.

Once he removed the viscera, Mikolu took a kidney and tossed it high up into the thorny branches of one of the tall acacias that hung over the huge rocks that formed the island. This was his gift of thanks to Kongai for a successful hunt. He put the heart aside for himself and took the rest of the entrails to the edge of the pit. To his surprise, Kifri was waiting for him looking up at him with her slanted eyes, her ears erect making her brow more wrinkled. This time she did not raise her back hair at him nor did she snarl a threat. He dropped the viscera into the pit and she immediately snatched part of it and dragged it to the far side to devour.

Mikolu smiled. It was a small victory, but it was still a victory. He looked down at her water bowl. It was almost empty. He knelt down, pulled it up by its thong and refilled it from his egg. Then, he carefully lowered it to the bottom of the pit, keeping the bowl as level and steady as possible so not much would spill out. He noticed Kifri was watching his every move as he worked. "See. I bring you the gifts of life, food and water, Kifri. We are meant to hunt as one and live together," he said gently to her and stood up.

She flicked her ears at his voice, but kept on eating, watching him in a suspicious manner. He went back to the Pranga fawn carcass and cut a portion of meat for himself from the haunch. He then took a branch from the pile he kept for the fires and carved a point on one end with a few skilled passes of his stone knife. This end he poked through the meat and placed over the fire, anchoring the opposite end of the branch between two rocks at the rim of the fire and piled small stones around it to hold it.

While it cooked, he walked to the edge of the huge boulder on which his camp was perched and looked out over the tops of the fever trees across the vast golden plains. Many Bush Things grazed in the distance and winged Bush Things soared in the sky above. He hoped the great herds would drift closer so that Kur would be drawn to them when he hunted again and not driven by hunger to search the rock island. He knew there was little danger from Kur during the day. But, the half-light time of the setting or rising of T'chuka's eye and the darkness of night belonged to Kur and all his kind.

Mikolu took a long nap after his meal. As darkness took the sky from the T'chuka's eye and a chill spread over the land, Mikolu awakened. Immediately he began tending the fires as the distant roars of Rowa reached him from over the plains announcing the time of the hunters had begun. He made sure his slingshot was at hand with plenty of stones large enough to discourage Kur. All night he remained alert, listening to the Bush Things out on the dark plains and watching the night sky.

He heard the pounding of hooves and barking of Raaha and knew something was hunting close by. When he heard the calls of a female Rowa to her cubs, he knew the hunt had been successful. With a clan of Rowa around, Kur would be cautious. Mikolu hoped the Rowa clan would move on with the herd. The clans of Kur and Rowa were blood enemies and if the huge cats stayed too long, they would force Kur to hunt among the rocks for game. Mikolu knew only too well that this could lead to a confrontation neither he or Kifri could handle at the moment.

Only when T'chuka brought back the light did Mikolu begin to relax. He cut some meat from the carcass and walked to the edge of the pit. Again, Kifri was waiting and looked up at him. To Mikolu's great joy she wagged her tail at him briefly before he dropped the meat to her. She still cast him suspicious glances, but she did not take the meat to the other side of the pit when he pulled up the water bowl to refill it. Instead, she ate it right where he had dropped it.

He spent that morning gathering dried branches in the fever tree forest and slept away the afternoon heat. When the chill of the coming night awakened Mikolu, he

found his fires were nearly out. Frantically he rushed from
fire to fire with the branches and sticks he had gathered.
He placed them carefully and stirred up the embers coax-
ing the flames until they licked hungrily at the bleached
wood. In the comforting glare of the cookfire, Mikolu
cooked his evening meal and thought of tomorrow. There
was not much water left in his egg. Like it or not he would
have to go to the spring.

With the first light of the new day, Mikolu left the rocky
island and entered the fever tree grove. At a slow, easy pace
he walked past a herd of M'Pranga, impalas. The red-
brown antelope with back swept horns raised their heads
to watch his passing.

Alert to the least movement in the grass or turn of a
leaf, Mikolu made his way toward the spring. The early
morning sun's glare off the rocks made him squint. He
passed the big fig tree hung with deep shadows. The light,
airy song of a bird burst forth from the branches high over
his head, telling him all was well here and that the shadows held no enemies. Not far beyond the fig he could smell
the wet earth scent of the spring. Soon he could hear the
familiar gentle gurgle of running water.

As he entered the miniature canyon, he startled a small
herd of Raaha. He had to dodge out of the way as the panicked animals rushed past him in a confusing blur of black
and white stripes so close that if he reached out his hand
he could have touched one. With greater caution, Mikolu
stalked toward the water's edge over mud full of the foot
prints of many Bush Things. He pulled the grass plug from
his bottle. As he knelt at the edge of the water he saw
them—the tracks of Kur in the muddy earth. They were
fresh.

Mikolu looked about him. There was no sign of Kur,
but he knew he could no longer stay at his camp. He held
the egg under the water and waited for it to fill, his heart

pounding in his chest. It seemed to take forever. As soon as it was full, he left the spring and headed straight for his camp at a jog.

He would have to free Kifri from the pit, now. He knew, that he would have to climb in to get her out. He knew, too, she could bite him badly enough to cripple him and keep him from hunting, but he would have to risk it. There was no way now that he would leave her trapped in the pit for Kur to kill. Nendaka had told him not too long ago that the Gods brought many tests into the life of each man. He told Mikolu, too, that many tests he would face would be harder than others because of the path he had begun. At first, Mikolu had not understood what he meant, but now he knew. This was one test from Kongai that he must not . . . would not fail.

As he climbed the boulder to his camp, Mikolu gathered his courage about him like a hide cloak. There could be no second thoughts, no doubts to dull his reactions. Upon reaching his camp, he cut a chunk of meat from the fawn carcass and walked to the edge of the pit.

He looked down at Kifri. Their eyes met. Knowing from experience and Mika's teachings it meant a threat to stare too long in the eyes of any meat eater, Mikolu looked away. When he carefully sat down, put his brown legs over the edge and slid in, the B'sengi backed to the far corner gurgling a strange call that sounded almost like a growl.

Ready to pull back out of her reach, Mikolu gingerly held the meat out to her. He kept a short distance from her, not wanting her to feel cornered. She stared at him, the hair on her back raising. She took a step toward him, hesitated, then lunged for the meat.

The second her jaws closed on the meat, Mikolu let go of it. He grabbed her by the scruff of the neck and base of her tail hoisting her over his head to the edge of the pit. She squirmed in his hands, pushing herself away from him by kicking his head and shoulders with her hind feet. Her blunt hind claws raked his face. Uttering a sound between clenched teeth that was more a scream than growl, she wriggled out of his grip and was gone in a heart beat.

CHAPTER *8*

FIRST HUNT

S he was gone. Heart filled with grief over losing Kifri and his dream, Mikolu took a strong grip on the rough, rocky rim of the pit and hauled himself out. He looked longingly out over the golden expanse of the plains for a glimpse of her. Nothing moved in the grass but a small herd of Pranga. Mikolu felt a desolation settle about him like a dust cloud. At least, he told himself, now she could just as easily escape from Kur. He would miss her but he had to go on about survival without her.

With most of the day ahead of him, Mikolu gathered

up his sling and stones and went hunting for his evening meal. He found a flock of T'woo in the tall grass among the fever trees and quickly dispatched one. Then, he gathered up more dead branches to refuel his cookfire.

As twilight muted the dusky colors of day to blues and grays, Mikolu put the bird in the cookfire. While the feathers seared off and the meat cooked he watched the evening eye of T'chuka rise over the trees and listened to the night sounds. He noticed the eye had begun to close. In a few more cycles it would be gone from the night sky as T'chuka slept. He prayed to Kongai that he would live to see it open again.

As he ate the succulent meat he looked over at the empty pit. It made him feel so alone now. He would leave this place when T'chuka brought the dawn.

He was finishing his meal, when he heard the light tick of claws on the rocky incline to his camp. His heart racing, he put the meat down and grabbed his slingshot and a few stones in his greasy hands. Quickly he loaded it and waited breathless, knowing it could be anything. He had a feeling that whatever it was, it was hungry and might be big enough to make a meal of him.

In the weak light of the stars and T'chuka's eye something small paused beyond the light of his fire. Two tiny points of green light told Mikolu that whatever it was, it was small and looking at him, studying him. Could it be Owa, or dare he even hope Kifri? He slowly put the slingshot down and broke off a meaty thigh from the fowl. This he tossed toward the eyes, but so it would land within the circle of light cast by the fire.

He saw a flash of white paws as Kifri crept cautiously into the light, snatched the meat and dashed away into the darkness. He smiled. So she had not found her clan and now considered him her provider of food. This very thought lead to a more dangerous decision. He would stay

for one more night and see if she truly would come to him
again of her own free will.

Mikolu tended his fire and dozed lightly throughout
the night always a part of him conscious to the noises
around him that might warn of Kur. Only when T'chuka
returned did he allow himself to fall into a deep sleep.
When a scolding bird awakened him to a world of bright
light and deep shadows, he looked about yawning and
stretching. Not far from his fire he noticed the splintered
thigh bone of the T'woo. Kifri had stayed close during the
night. She had probably found it more comfortable to sleep
on the sun warmed rock than the grass below the huge boulders. It could even be that she found it safer to stay near
him not having the protection of the pack. Mikolu knew
that if she were among her own clan she would have slept
in a pile of other dogs each finding comfort in the touch
of the others. It was their habit to all snuggle together for
security and to ward off the night chill. He had seen a litter of pups do this under a tree he had slept in the first
night Mika had sent him into the bush alone in prepara-
tion for the Long Walk. She must miss her clan as much as
he missed his, Mikolu thought. It could be this very need
for companionship that would make her accept him.

Mikolu spent the morning hunting T'woo and this
time managed to shoot down two. When he returned to
his camp high in the rocks he found Kifri sitting a bow
shot from the smoldering fire. She watched him add
branches to the fire from his supply pile of wood to the
side. He used his stone knife to cut open the birds and
pulled out the entrails. He tossed a liver toward her. She
quickly picked it up and devoured it. He tossed the rest of
the entrails so they landed a little closer to himself. She
approached, eyeing him suspiciously and quickly ate the
second offering.

Then, Mikolu held out the liver of the other bird.

"Come, Kifri. I will not hurt you," he said in a quiet, gentle voice.

She crept closer. She moved cautiously, her weight on the very tips of her toes ready to bolt, her tail slowly wagging. Mikolu remained still and watched her without staring into her eyes. She stopped her advance an arms length from his outstretched hand and gurgled a strange trilling call at him. Then, slowly, ever so slowly she stretched her neck out, her feet planted firmly, ready to bolt away. She gingerly took the liver from his fingers in a slow bite, snagging it with her incisors. Mikolu still did not move as she pulled away with the liver and bolted it down.

In a slow smooth move, he picked up one of the T'woo and held it out to her by a leg. Again, Kifri made her slow-motion approach. This time when she grabbed the dangling neck, Mikolu did not release his hold so quickly. With her attention on the T'woo, he got his free hand out and ran it down her side pushing her trust to the limit. When her ears flicked back, he let the T'woo go.

Kifri proudly trotted to a patch of shade with her prize. She dropped it on the rock, pinned it down with her front paws and began pulling the feathers from it eyeing him suspiciously, but without fear. Mikolu tossed his T'woo on the fire to cook quite satisfied with himself. When his own stomach was full, he piled more branches on the fire and licked the grease from his fingers. Kifri lay down on the very edge of the firelight watching him when she was not napping. The calls of the night insects and the warmth of the fire soon lulled him into a light sleep.

The next morning he was awakened by birdsong and a tickle on his forehead. He opened his eyes to slits to find Kifri's nose in his face. She was sniffing at him. He lay as still as he could so he wouldn't scare her. Yet, somehow he felt she knew he was awake. He was sure of it when she poked him with a front paw.

He sat up slowly. She bolted away, swung around and faced him in a play bow resting her forequarters on the rock with her rump in the air and tail wagging slowly. She tilted her head up and called, "O-o-o-o-o-w-a-a-a! R-o-o-o!"

As he rose to his feet she circled him remaining out of his reach.

"Kifri," he said in a quiet voice and reached out for her.

She dodged away and continued to circle wider around him.

Mikolu pulled his hand back and kept it at his side. Perhaps she thought the outstretched arm a threat. "Kifri", he called again and tried to imitate her strange trilling call.

She bounded over to him her lips pulled back in a crazy puppy grin and jumped up and down on him, punching him with her front paws and gurgling her strange call. It was a greeting call, Mikolu knew, and her antics were part of a pack greeting. His patience had been rewarded. He crouched down so as not to appear so large and threatening and gently reached out to briefly touch her back. She allowed it and he was thrilled. She jumped and danced back and forth, wagging her curled tail, poking him with her cold, wet nose and slapping at him with her front paws in play as if he was another B'sengi. Her joyful mood was contagious.

Mikolu got up and they began a wild game of tag across the giant boulders, down into the fever tree grove and the tall grass that grew in the open areas between the trees. Kifri hid from him several times only to suddenly jump out from a clump of grass or from behind a fallen tree to tag him with a gentle nip on the knee or calf of his leg. Once she ran between his legs and tripped him so bad that he fell sprawling in the grass. He laughed so hard that he almost lost his breath and tears came to his eyes.

The play ended abruptly when Kifri suddenly went into a crouch. Head level with her shoulders, she began to stalk towards a rock slide at the foot of the rock island by a huge acacia tree. Instantly, Mikolu was alert and looked in the direction Kifri was headed.

Eeka, the hyraxes, small animals that vaguely resembled a hare with a chunky body, pointed face with long whiskers and small round ears were basking on the sun warmed rocks or hopping about eating fallen acacia seed pods. The whole colony seemed to be making their home in the rock slide. Mikolu knew if he could get two, they would be enough food to start the journey away from the rock island and Kur.

Mikolu crouched low, loading his slingshot and followed Kifri using every tree and scrubby thorn bush as cover approaching down wind. Kifri continued to move with her head level with her shoulders and ears pointed forward, stalking more like a big cat. She stopped and froze still as a shadow any time an Eeka looked her way. Mikolu imitated her. When she was a quarter of a bow shot from the colony, she suddenly sprang forward and rushed them at a full run. Mikolu ran too, ready to release a stone at the first clear target.

The high pitched, screeching alarm calls of the scattering Eeka echoed off the rocks. Many of the Eekas retreated into holes and cracks between the rocks. Kifri did not bother with these. She suddenly veered in her mad dash to cut several off from their retreat. She forced them to climb the big acacia to the lower branches and had enough momentum herself to follow them up the slanted trunk.

One ran along the branch. Mikolu deftly let fly his stone and shot the Eeka right out of the tree. Kifri was after it the second it hit the ground. She quickly ran down the trunk, grabbed the stunned Eeka by the neck and shook it. Mikolu expected her to run off with her kill, but instead she dropped it and yodeled. She allowed him to approach and pick it up.

"Good, Kifri. See? I told you we will hunt together," he said to her looking deep into her slanted brown eyes. "Now we must get one more so we can leave this place." He tucked the limp Eeka under his belt. Then, he headed for a thick patch of brush not far from the acacia tree and hid. Kifri was right on his heels.

Here they waited down wind for the colony to get over its fear and return to feeding. Kifri sat at his side her ears cocked forward and every muscle tense. Her attention was on the tree again. Mikolu, too, watched with another stone ready to fly. At the sound of small claws scrabbling on bark, he tensed.

An Eeka was suddenly in full view in the shadows at the base of the tree. Mikolu stood up quickly and let the stone fly. He knocked the Eeka right off its feet and Kifri was on it in a heartbeat. She grabbed it by the neck and shook it, then dropped it. Mikolu walked over, picked it up and tucked it under his belt. With Kifri right on his heels, he climbed back up to his camp. The fires had burned out. He gathered up his egg shell and stone knife and they left the rock island for the vast grassy plain that surrounded it.

With only half a day left, Mikolu thought it best to seek out the safest place he knew to make camp for the night. That place was the very acacia tree from which he had first watched the dog pack at the beginning of his Long Walk.

As they left the acacia grove at the base of the rock island and started across the sea of grass, Kifri followed at his side or bounded through the tall grass ahead of him like a Pranga. He watched her with a joyful heart. As he walked he thanked Kongai for the gift of her friendship and prayed that they would stay together.

He got part of the answer in her eyes. Each time she ran ahead of him she would go as far as a bow shot, then stop and look back over her shoulder as if to make sure he was still following. Each time she did this, her eyes spoke of a loyalty that humbled him. She had accepted him as her new clan member.

T'chuka's eye was a red orb flickering in the heat waves low on the horizon by the time they reached the huge, solitary acacia that stood like a sentinel on the plains. Mikolu cautiously circled it once, staring into the shadows of its huge branches to make sure no danger hid there. Then he set about gathering the fallen branches and twigs that lay scattered about so that he could build a fire. He piled them on the location of his original fire pit. Soon the growing darkness was alive with the flames of his cookfire. He tossed Kifri one of the Eeka and put the other in the fire to scorch off the fur and cook at the same time.

Kifri took her Eeka to the very edge of the firelight and settled next to a large clump of tall grass to devour it. Crunching bones, she cast an occasional glance at Mikolu. When Mikolu judged his share of the catch to be done, he used a stick to remove the charred carcass from the flames. He broke it open with his stone knife to cool. As the night settled around him and insect song and the calls of T'heeah and Owa drifted over the plains, Mikolu began his meal.

Kifri got up and settled closer to him, staring at him, her eyes following the motion of his hands as he broke off bits of meat and ate around the bones. Curious to see if she would accept cooked red meat as easily as fowl, he tossed her part of the hind leg with the bone still in it. She picked it up, spit it out, pawed at it and carried it off to her eating spot in the grass. Mikolu giggled at her strange re-action trying to keep from choking on a mouthful of meat. She came back to sit in front of him again as he finished the last bits of meat on the back.

"You have had yours. But, if you want the bones you can have them," he said gently to her.

She stood up, the hair down her back suddenly going erect and she snarled.

It took Mikolu a moment to notice her eyes were focused on something behind him. He scrambled to his feet turning his back to the fire and stared into the darkness.

Just beyond the reach of the firelight green eyes glowed, and there came from the darkness a low rumbling. It was Kur!

Heart hammering in his chest, Mikolu grabbed a burning branch from the fire and hurled it at the big cat. A sharp snarl split the air. Kifri snarled and backed towards the tree. The glowing eyes disappeared.

Mikolu breathed easier. Yet, he knew even with the fire it would not be totally safe. Kur would be close by maybe waiting for it to burn out. Mikolu added a few more branches and part of a broken limb to keep it burning through the night. The fire licked skyward growing in intensity. Mikolu then headed for the massive leaning trunk of the acacia and climbed to the crotch where two thick limbs three times the girth of his own body grew out from the main trunk. Though Kur could climb, the fire blazing so close to the tree would greatly discourage him from trying.

"Kifri, come," he called and slapped the tree limb. "I have seen you climb. You can reach me."

The B'sengi looked up at him and whined. She circled the tree several times growing more frantic.

"Kifri, come. You can do it," he called again.

She looked up at him and yodeled. Then she ran away into the darkness and his heart sank. Suddenly she was back, streaking past the fire in a blur of golden-red and white. She ran up the tree trunk to him and he had to grab her to keep her from falling. He hugged her to him and she licked his face.

Together they watched the tiny fires in the sky that lit the way to the Hidden World and listened to the night voices. With Kur around there would be little sleep for them both except for short naps. Mikolu settled in with his back against one of the massive limbs with Kifri across his lap. He gently stroked her silky back and saw her head drop to rest on her outstretched front legs. Soon his eyes grew heavy and he dozed. The distant roars of Rowa clan went hardly noticed at all.

CHAPTER 9

THE JUDGMENT

Mikolu was awakened at first light by the thunder of hooves and Kifri shifting nervously on his lap. He opened his eyes to a stampeding herd of Rhaha galloping past his tree. He quickly spotted the cause.

A large pack of Hoori, the blotchy-coated, bat eared wild dogs was running the herd in a tight circle. There were more dogs than Mikolu had fingers. These wild dogs

were fierce hunters three times the size of Kifri and capable
of taking large game. Even Kur feared to be caught on open
ground by the Hoori clan. Mikolu was not about to try to leave
the tree until they were gone.

Though there were foals in the Rhaha herd the dogs
had singled out a pregnant mare. When the herd scattered,
the dogs closed in streaming along at high speed in the
copper light of dawn. Almost immediately the mare fell
behind the herd and then gave up, standing motionless as
one dog grabbed her nose. Other dogs caught up and
ripped at her pregnant belly. They surged at her with such
force that the flesh of her uplifted hind quarters quivered
in the striped skin. The mare seemed entirely docile, un-
afraid. Mikolu knew that when death was near a herd animal would rarely defend itself with hooves and teeth used
so effectively in battling with its own kind, though such
resistance might well save its life. The Rhaha still stood after her entrails had been snatched out, then sagged down
dead. Her unborn colt was dragged into the clear and torn
apart and devoured off to one side.

The morning was still except for the wet sound of the
eating Hoori. Mikolu hugged Kifri to keep her from leaving the tree. After the blood-stained dogs filled their bel-
lies and licked each other clean, they left the carcass one
by one. When a single T'heea suddenly appeared, it was
driven off screaming hysterically in a violent attack of bites
to its rump. Mikolu dared not try to leave the tree until
the last dog left the carcass. Though there was still meat
left, Mikolu knew that in a day and a night when Rowa and
T'heea, the Korha clan of vultures, Owa, Tik and finally
Din the clan of carrion beetles had all finished, there would
be no sign but the stained, pressed grass that a death ever
took place. As the last dog disappeared over a low hill
Mikolu and Kifri left their perch.

In the days that followed, Mikolu learned the various

ways Kifri hunted and how to read her moods by observing carefully how she carried herself and at what angle she held her ears. He found that she, like all B'sengi, took advantage of circumstance. It was her clan's secret to survival and what had lead her to adopt him so quickly as a pack member. At times she drove small game and birds to him. Other times she caught and killed game herself and waited for him to catch up to her after the chase. Though he did dig roots and snack on grubs, he was never without meat for the rest of his "Long Walk" and he never had to risk scavenging from any large predator's kill.

Soon T'chuka's night eye was almost fully open. It was time to return to the Sacred Baobab tree to meet his clan. The ghost child was dead and a man was now ready to come out of the world of Bush Things. But, unlike all that had gone before him, Mikolu was bringing with him a Bush Thing and this Bush Thing came of its own free will. There was much magic in all this. Mikolu could feel it. He knew old Nendaka would feel it too. It made him wonder of the special path Nendaka had mentioned that he was to travel. Perhaps it was his dream come true with Kifri and she the prophesied Gift he would bring to the clan. Yet, he felt deep inside that there might be more. Old Nendaka, as mysterious as he was wise never did reveal all of what he saw in his visions at once.

As they crossed the last open expanse of the plains before the dry riverbed that would lead them to the tree, Kifri became excited about a scent. She began running back and forth in front of Mikolu, her nose to the ground. She stopped now and then to stand on her hind feet to peer over the tops of the grass at a distant herd of Pranga. Mikolu knew she was on to something close and slipped a stone into his sling. It would fulfill the last demand of his Long Walk, that he bring back meat. The gift of food would mean even more if the two of them returned to the clan with game he got with her help. It would go a long way toward proving how a joining of the clans of men and B'sengi could be good for both.

Kifri suddenly broke away from him at a run and dived at something in a large clump of tall grass. A young Pranga leaped up, staggered and took off at an awkward, limping run toward the herd. It was not a small fawn, but of an age where it was no longer in need of its mother's milk. By the lurching way the Pranga ran, Mikolu could tell it was lame.

Kifri ran after it and grabbed it by one ear as she passed, throwing it off balance so that it fell. Mikolu did not have a stone big enough to kill it and he feared he might hit Kifri if he tried to strike the antelope in the head to stun it. So, he pulled his stone knife from his belt, wishing he had the bow and arrows of manhood. He ran, but by the time he reached the Pranga it had shaken off Kifri and was on its feet again and running. Kifri immediately chased it. This time she grabbed its tail in her teeth, stiffened her legs and pulled back to slow it down.

Mikolu ran as fast as he could to catch up to them. The young Pranga bucked and kicked out with its sharp hind hooves. Kifri deftly dodged them, but she was forced to let go. As the Pranga scrambled for better balance, Kifri leaped for its head to grab an ear again. It bleated in terror as Mikolu caught up to the struggle.

Mikolu threw himself on the back of the Pranga, pulling the thrashing animal over on its side with Kifri still hanging on a twisted ear. They rolled in a confusion of kicking hooves, tangle of legs and dust. Mikolu ended up under the Pranga with Kifri still hanging on, her jaws inches from his own face. Quickly, Mikolu threw one arm around the Pranga's neck and with his free hand plunged the knife into its throat to sever the jugular and windpipe. He could hardly see what he was doing, but felt warm blood and heard the death gurgle of the Pranga. In moments it

stopped its wild struggling and went limp. Kifri released her
hold on the ear and stood staring at him as he lay breathless
hugging the dead Bush Thing, his face pressed against the
back of its head. He sat up, pushing the limp Pranga off
himself.

Kifri stared at him. Then she pointed her nose to the
sky and yodeled, "O-o-o-o! O-o-o-o! O-o-o-r-r-r!."

It was a sound he had come to recognize as her victory
call. Mikolu burst out laughing and tried to imitate her
yodel. Immediately she was jumping all over him, licking
his face and wagging her curled tail so hard he thought it
would fall off and jump around by itself. Finally in control
of his laughter, Mikolu got up off the ground. He cut an
ear from the carcass and left it on a thorn bush no taller
than his knees as an offering to Kongai. He took a thong
from his belt pouch and tied the left hind and front leg
together to make the Pranga easier to carry, and slung the
carcass over his shoulders like a heavy cape. Pleased with
the results of their hunt, Mikolu continued the journey to
the Sacred Baobab tree with Kifri bounding ahead of him
through the tall grass.

As he passed through land he began to recognize, his
thoughts turned to the possibility of Kifri not accepting
the other members of the clan. She was skittish and had to
be to survive in a land of dangerous predators. Would this
lead her to bite in defense if a much larger adult clan
member moved too quickly toward her? The darker as-
pect of B'sengi wild ways made him worry. He decided he
would have to be alert to her every move and posture to
avoid a bad experience and be ready to shield and comfort her so she would not be afraid. He worried most of all
about the jealous Shonga.

Soon T'chuka's burning eye was high in the sky devouring the shadows on the land and the heat prickled his
skin. In the distant heat waves the Sacred Baobab shim-

mered and Mikolu could make out several small dark blobs moving about. Mikolu knew it was his clan waiting for him camped beyond the sacred tree and his heart was filled with joy.

Several of the shadows headed out toward him and quickly congealed into familiar clan members. Turu was the first to reach him. He slowed and hesitated at the sight of Kifri.

"She is a friend and has decided to stay with me, Turu. It is Kongai's gift to me. We caught this Pranga together," Mikolu announced with pride as Mika came up behind Turu. Kifri drew closer to Mikolu, her back hair up in warning and she rumbled deep in her throat. Mikolu stopped and stretched his arm out to touch her. "Be still. No one will harm you." He turned to Turu. "Do not move too fast. She has never met anyone of our clan but me."

Turu stopped his advance, yet smiled broadly, his white, even teeth brightening his usually serious expression. "I knew you would some day fulfill your wish with the help of Kongai. This must be the Gift Nendaka spoke of."

Mika cast Kifri a long suspicious look. "You look well," Mika said and put his hand on Mikolu's shoulder. "And this Bush Thing has not tried to eat your toes off?"

Kifri quickly moved to Mikolu's opposite side rumbling to herself, but did not bolt.

"No, Uncle. She is Kifri, a true friend. If it were not for her, I would not be so well fed. Not once did I have to scavenge old meat from Rowa. I think if everyone treats her as I have, she will be everyones friend and help us hunt with more success." He handed the Pranga to Mika. He wanted his hands free so he could defend Kifri. He knew Shonga would make trouble.

Mika nodded in approval, but his eyes still held a dark suspicion and did not quite leave Kifri. Kifri was equally suspicious and it showed in the way she carried her tail uncurled and down and the tenseness of her every muscle. They all headed toward the huge tree. As they drew closer to the Sacred Baobab the others of the clan gathered about them, but not as close as they normally would for Kifri stayed close to Mikolu's legs and growled. Old Nendaka stood apart from the others leaning on his carved wood staff and smiled knowingly at Mikolu, a twinkle in his eye. "Did I not say your path would be different than all those who went before you? See, you have brought the Gift. And the Bush Things have told me more, Mikolu. You speak with them and understand them in ways other men do not. Your way is one of a special magic. But, we will discuss this at a later time when you are ready."

Kifri growled louder.

"S-h-h-h-h-h! Do not be afraid, Kifri. This is my clan," Mikolu said gently to her and stooped down to stroke her silky coat. This seemed to calm her. She let her hair go flat and stopped rumbling.

Waku, a Rowa skin draped about his powerful shoulders, eyed them both with no expression. "I see you have brought back a gift of food. And what is this? A live Bush Thing of the B'sengi clan?"

"The Bush Thing has a name, Great Waku," Mikolu said with pride. "She is Kifri and she is a true friend. It is she who saw I was not without fresh meat after I rescued her from a deep pit among giant boulders." But, his pride was a short lived pride for he saw Shonga push through the crowd. Shonga was carrying his spear point down as if he were about to use it. By the look of disdain in his eyes, his opinion of Mikolu and his dream had not changed. "We do not need this Bush Thing among us. It will draw Kur into our midst. Let me kill it now so that our children may remain safe from the jaws of Kur." He raised his spear.

Waku stepped in front of Shonga and angrily pushed the spear aside. "Young fool. It is not up to you to decide this matter. I will discuss this with the Elders and it is we who shall decide if the Bush Thing of the B'sengi clan may live among us."

Shonga lowered his spear, but his eyes still burned like those of Kur. He nodded his head respectfully and averted his eyes from Waku's cold stare. Then Waku walked with the three oldest hunters and Nendaka to the shade of the Sacred Baobab tree. All sat down cross-legged at the foot of the huge, bloated trunk to discuss the matter. Shonga stalked off in anger to join his young wife and son of two seasons at their cook fire in the camp just beyond the tree. As Mika headed toward his cook fire, Mikolu stayed with Turu and Kifri in the sparse shade cast by a thorn bush. Many in the clan eyed Kifri with suspicion, daring not to come too close. Mikolu squatted down beside her and stroked her head and back to calm her. Turu watched.

"How did you find her?" he asked.

"Her night cries told me what direction. I found her trapped in a pit of boulders," Mikolu answered not taking his eyes off Kifri who in turn was intently watching Turu. Her ears were up, but Mikolu could feel a tenseness in her muscles.

"How did you get her to stay with you?" Turu went on and slowly squatted down next to Mikolu and the wary B'sengi.

"I fed her and brought her water and spoke to her. She soon saw that I was her friend," Mikolu answered. "We were together many days before I took her out of the pit. She ran away, but she came back. She stayed with me and we hunted together. We are the same clan now."

"Will she let me touch her as you do?" Turu asked, his eyes bright and pleading.

"I don't know. But, we can try. Give me your hand," Mikolu said. His words were brave, but he was not sure.

Turu slowly held out his hand. Kifri looked at him and

put her ears back. Her hair raised down her back and she pressed her body close to Mikolu. Turu began to slowly withdraw his hand, but Mikolu took it firmly. Kifri pricked up her ears and sniffed at both their hands. Turu's eyes widened.

"See, Kifri, Turu is my friend, too. And he can be your friend," Mikolu said gently. He placed both their hands on her shoulder. She turned her head to sniff both arms. Mikolu felt the tickle of her whiskers. Her tail curled and wagged slowly.

Turu giggled at her. She licked both their arms as Mikolu released his hold on Turu's hand. Turu laughed harder, lost his balance and fell back on his behind. Mikolu laughed until tears ran from his eyes. Kifri put her head back and crowed, "O-o-o-o! R-o-o-o-o! O-o-o-o!" Then she ran around them in crazy circles.

When Mikolu got control of himself, he asked, "Do you think the Elders will let her stay?"

Turu sat up and his face grew serious. "I truly do not know. Nothing like this has ever happened. There could be danger here. She could bite someone or Shonga could attack her and end up dividing the clan into those who want her and those who do not."

Mikolu nodded not knowing how to answer. Kifri did pose some problems and he knew he had to confront them. He prayed to Kongai that he would not have to choose between his clan and Kifri.

They both went silent. Kifri settled next to Mikolu and started to doze. They waited and waited. The shadows grew long and the women started their cook fires. Then, the Elders and Waku stood up and walked over to Mikolu followed by many of the clan who wished to hear the outcome of such a lengthy deliberation.

"The matter has been decided in fairness," Waku announced. "Since all do not agree on allowing a Bush

Thing to live among us, Mikolu, it is up to you to prove the worth of Kifri. She is to be tied out on a thong away from the camp over night. You may stay with her and build a fire to keep the Bush Things away. If she is not taken by Kur or another Bush Thing, or does not chew through the thong and run away during the night she can join us in the morning on an Oom hunt for your feast of manhood," Waku explained looking deep into Mikolu's eyes. "And now you are to receive the tools of manhood."

Mikolu stood up as Mika came through the small crowd, holding the bow, arrows and spear he had made, but the joy and pride Mikolu knew he should feel was absent. There was only pain in his heart. To tie Kifri out beyond the safety of the fires was like a death banishment used only to punish the most serious of crimes against the clan. Kifri had done nothing to warrant such treatment. Even if Kur did not come, he was sure Shonga would sneak out and kill Kifri himself out of jealousy with a well placed arrow. He choked back the hurt and graciously accepted the tools his uncle had made for him. Regardless of the judgment, he was determined not to let those who were against him win no matter how much power they had in the clan. Kongai, Lord of Bush Things and the hunt had bestowed a gift of the friendship of a Bush Thing and he was going to see that it was accepted by the clan of men. Mikolu knew well from Nendaka's teachings that one did not refuse the gift of a God.

CHAPTER 10

NIGHT OF THE HUNTER

Mikolu sat glumly by the family cook fire with his uncle Mika and Shana, his mother. He did not feel like eating the evening meal though he knew he needed to eat something to have strength for the hunt tomorrow. As far as he was concerned there was no tomorrow without Kifri. When his mother handed him his share of the Pranga meat in a wood bowl he ate only a few mouthfuls, then gave the rest to Kifri.

When he looked over at Mika, he found his uncle

watching him. "I feel your desolation, Mikolu, but the elders
have spoken and you will obey them," Mika said. "You are a
man now, bound by the laws of the clan. There is some danger here on this new path you have put us on."

"I know," Mikolu said in a low voice. Then a gloomy
silence fell over them all as they ate.

At the end of the meal Mika handed him a long rope
of braided hide. Sadly he took Kifri beyond the light of
the fires. When he looked back to see just how far he had
gone from his family's fire he saw Shonga watching him as
if to make sure he carried out the elders' order. He found
a stake in the ground about a bow shot away near thorn
bushes and tied one end of the rope to it.

"I am sorry, Kifri. The elders wish this to be done," he
said gently as he tied the other end around her neck. He
stroked her silky coat and hugged her, fighting back tears
that threatened to come. A man did not cry, but he was no
longer so sure he was a man if others could so easily take
something away from him. He prayed that Kongai would
protect her.

When he stood up and walked away from her to fetch
wood for their fire, she whimpered and followed him to
the very end of her rope. Then she screamed a near human cry of frustration. Mikolu turned to look from her to
Shonga. Shonga glared at him, then turned away and
walked to his fire where his wife and small son waited. A
heaviness in his heart, Mikolu continued his walk back to
his uncle's fire, Kifri's cries haunting his every step.

Mika was not sitting by the fire. When Mikolu stepped
into the welcomed fire light, his mother paused in repair-
ing a small basket of woven grass and looked up at him. "I
know you are hurting inside, Mikolu, but she will be all
right. The B'sengi are a clever clan."

"They can only be clever when allowed to be free, not
when tied at the end of a thong rope," Mikolu protested

as he picked up some wood from a pile by the fire listening
to Kifri's eerie spirit calls. Her calls sent a chill up his back
and he noticed others of the clan often looking out into the
darkness, white showing in their eyes like frightened Bush
Things. Perhaps, Mikolu thought, some fear the Gods might
be angered by this action on the part of the elders of testing
the worth of a gift.

As he carried an armful of branches toward Kifri he
caught sight of old Nendaka. He was walking with Mika
through the darkness toward their fire aided by a staff
carved with geometric markings and ending in a Rowa's
head. Nendaka's gray hair was silvered in T'chuka's light
and the Kur skin cape he wore over his shoulder seemed
to take on a life of its own in the cold light. "She calls upon
Kongai for protection as all hunters do, Mikolu. She is a
charmed one," he said as he passed close. "The others in
the clan will soon realize this. The bones have spoken so."
He held out and shook the pouch of his oracle bones
handed down to him by his father. Then, he continued on
his way to his own cook fire.

"Listen to Nendaka, Mikolu," Mika said as he sat by
the fire. "I asked him to read the bones. Do not worry.
They spoke of a great test passed. Build your fire and get
some sleep. You will need to be alert for the hunt. We will
leave before the sun rises."

Mikolu did not answer. He sighed and walked to Kifri.
Kifri had stopped calling. She jumped up on him the moment he reached her. He dropped the wood and paused
to scratch her ears. Then, he set about digging a shallow
fire pit with his stone knife and placed the branches in it.
Kifri watched him as he returned to his uncle's fire for a
small flaming branch. He came back and poked it into
the pile of branches. As the dried wood caught the flame
and the fire crackled to life, Kifri backed away and sat down
on her haunches.

Mikolu then returned to his uncle's fire to retrieve his slingshot and bag of stones so he could drive away any unwelcome Bush Things. If it was light, he would have brought his bow and arrows, but he knew all he would see of Bush Things in the dark would be glowing eyes. To try to shoot one in the dark was not wise. If Kur showed and was wounded with an arrow it would put everyone in grave danger. It would only anger the great cat and make him more ferocious.

Then with his slingshot and bag of stones clutched tightly in his hand Mikolu entered the darkness between the fires where the shadows made strange patterns on the silvered grass.

He heard Kifri's low growl before he saw her. She was half crouching in the black, tangled shadow of a thorn bush far beyond his small fire. Something else moved in the moon shadows not half a bow shot from her. It was low to the ground moving with a liquid grace silent as Death itself. It was Kur!

Mikolu's heart skipped a beat. Then, as Kifri backed slowly into the light of T'chuka's night eye he could see she had chewed through the thong and freed herself.

"No!" he cried out, loading a stone into his slingshot and in desperation letting it fly at the spotted cat.

It struck the big cat on the flank. Kur spun around snarling to face him, green eyes blazing with an inner fire. Mikolu knew he was looking into the eyes of death. He froze and wished he had thought to bring his spear instead of the weapon of a boy. His mistake would cause his death.

When Kur took a step toward him, Kifri was on the cat in a flash. She bit him on the tip of the tail. When he turned to swing at her with his claws she was gone. She ran around him in a circle, just out of range of his paws, dodging, charging weaving and snapping at him each chance she got. She danced the same dance of death as Merka, the mongoose and S'Ska, the cobra.

Her attack broke Mikolu's trance of fear. He loaded
his slingshot with a big stone and hit Kur again. This time
he struck the side of the cat's head with a resounding thunk.
Snarling, the cat backed toward the bushes. An arrow
plunged into the dirt at Kur's right paw. Hunters shouted
behind Mikolu. Kur practically turned himself inside out
as he made a sharp turn to retreat into the thorn bushes to
become invisible in the black shadows.

"Kifri", Mikolu called. She came to him in the firelight wagging her curled tail and gurgling her victory call
as Mika, Turu, Waku and Shonga came up behind him.

"It is the B'sengi that drew Kur," Shonga protested
shaking his fist at Kifri. "I told you she would bring danger.
Unless she is returned to the Bush Things this will always
happen and soon Kur will take our children."

"Kur could have easily been drawn by the smell of the
meat and followed Mikolu this morning across the grassland," Waku said sharply. "His territory is wide and covers
that of our clan and that of the River People."

Mikolu saw old Katuka push past several hunters. A
grin split his dark face and he said, "Kifri freed herself and
did not run away to leave Mikolu to face Kur alone. Anyone
who can help in driving Kur away as Kifri has done deserves
a place in the clan. I change my words at the Council and
say she should stay."

"Mikolu, move her to a place by your uncle's fire with
you. She will hunt with us in the morning and we will see
how useful she can prove herself," Waku said.

Shonga was about to protest. He took a deep breath,
but before he could start shouting in his vicious way, his
words were stopped by a glare from Waku.

Mikolu hugged Kifri and she let him pick her up to
carry her to his uncle's cookfire. As he carried her, she put a
front paw on each of his shoulders and licked his face and
ears making it very difficult for him to see where he was going.

CHAPTER *11*

GIFT OF KONGAI

The new day was just a yellow streak low on a gray horizon when the hunters left the camp in search of an Oom herd. They moved out in single file with their spears in hand Waku at the head of the line. Since he was as yet an unproven hunter of large game in the eyes of the clan Mikolu was last with Kifri at his side. Kifri stayed close to him and walked with her ears cocked back and her tail uncurled, betraying her mistrust of the other hunters in front of her.

Mikolu read her mood and could feel her tension. He was thankful she was keeping her distance from the others, especially Shonga.

Shonga was fifth in the line and had nothing but hateful looks for Kifri when they left camp. He refused to even acknowledge Mikolu's presence. Mikolu was quite surprised Shonga was even on the hunt. He could have refused to go and no one would have questioned him. He had made it quite plain in front of many how he felt about Kifri. But then, hunting Oom was dangerous. For one who fancied himself chief one day to miss displaying his hunting skills against such dangerous game would be a blow to his pride. It seem to Mikolu as if Shonga suddenly felt himself in a competition with him and the hated Bush Thing accompanying the other hunters of the clan. Mikolu knew none of them wanted to miss seeing if she would make hunting easier as he believed.

They walked most of the morning over the golden plains of waving grass. Thousands of Bush Things grazed in open country with hardly a tree upon it. The sun was almost overhead when a great herd of Oom was found at the edge of a muddy waterhole. They were noisy beasts, lowing and snorting as they moved to the water's edge for a turn to drink. Huge bulls with wide-spread horns guarded the flanks of the herd.

Waku held up his hand in a silent signal to stop. They all stood a long time observing the herd to pick out a likely target. Kifri stayed with Mikolu a small distance from the others. The hair down her back was up and it worried Mikolu. He quickly saw why. Shonga was headed his way.

"Wa! Wa! R-r-r-r-r-r!" Kifri barked in warning.

The young hunter stopped only close enough for his low voice to reach Mikolu. "I will show you we do not need

a Bush Thing to hunt with us." There was a show of teeth
when he talked and he pointed to Kifri with the sharp, stone
tip of his spear.

Mikolu only glared at Shonga. Shonga's hatred of Kifri
had to be as intense as a bush fire for him to use his voice
at such a time. Any man's voice might alert their quarry to
their presence and hunters only used silent hand signals
while stalking. The Oom ignored Kifri's bark. They had
no fear of such a small predator. Then Mikolu saw Waku
point silently to a young bull grazing some distance from
main body of the herd. Waku made a spear throwing motion with his hand. Mikolu understood that this animal was
the chosen target. Then, Waku pointed at each hunter and
indicated with a broad sweep of his hand who was to stalk
the animal and who was to wait in ambush.

The hunters split up. Half, including Mika, Mikolu and
Kifri, hid down wind crouching in the brush and behind
clumps of grass to wait for the others to drive the bull
towards them. The others with Waku, Turu and Shonga
stalked upwind of the grazing bull. Each time the bull
picked up his head to look around, the hunters froze in
their tracks. When he dropped his head to graze again,
they resumed stalking him. Soon the stalking hunters had
him half surrounded at a distance of a bow shot with his
only escape route towards the waiting hunters. Then, they
suddenly rushed him shouting and waving their arms.

The young bull bolted with a loud snort. However, he
did not retreat immediately. Instead, he swerved away from
Waku and charged Turu, narrowly missing him with his
horns. Turu was forced to dodge, tripped over a clump of
grass and fell. Shonga threw his spear at the bull. It sunk
into the animal's neck muscles. The sudden shock of pain
sent the young bull swerving toward Mikolu's group of
hunters. The bull turned so fast that Shonga's spear fell
out leaving a bloody wound.

Mikolu and the other hunters jumped up from their various hiding places, spears ready. Another spear was thrown, hit the bull in the shoulder, but struck bone and fell out. Mikolu did not see who had thrown it, but it caused the bull to veer again and this time it came directly at him and Kifri. Kifri darted out of the way as he side stepped the charging bull. With all the strength he could muster, Mikolu drove his own spear between its ribs half way down its right side. The spear was pulled from his hands as the powerful Bush Thing rushed past so close that he could feel its hot breath. Another spear flew past Mikolu, but missed the wounded bull. The herd was alerted now and had begun to stampede away from the hunt spreading a choking cloud of dust. The young bull kept running parallel to it and the hunting party followed half blinded by the dust.

Mikolu looked around for Kifri. One moment she had been beside him and the next moment lost in the dust cloud. As the cloud began to disperse, Mikolu caught sight of the wounded bull far ahead of the hunters. His spear was still stuck between its ribs and Kifri was after it in a ground consuming double suspension gallop. Normally the hunters would have to track a wounded Oom a day, sometimes two days, until it was too weak to flee further and made a stand for a final fight with deadly horns. They were lucky if larger predators like the Rowa or T'heea did not beat them to their wounded quarry. Kifri seemed ready to change their hunting method.

Hearing the shouts of the hunters, she nipped at the tail and heels of the young bull. Tormented by the spear still in his side, he turned on her and tried to gore her with his curved horns. Able to turn in a smaller circle than the bull, Kifri easily dodged his huge bulk. The spear fell out as the bull turned in a tight circle determined to catch the B'sengi. She retreated to a safe distance and ran in a circle around him in the opposite direction he was moving. He stopped, then changed direction after her for a few steps. Then, he cocked his ears toward the fast approaching hunters and slowly trotted toward his retreating herd. His wound was bleeding profusely and a red foam formed around his mouth. Kifri ran after him again.

Mikolu picked up his spear as the other hunters passed him shouting and howling. When Mikolu looked toward the bull he found that Kifri had grabbed it by the tail. He knew she was far too small to stop let alone kill the huge animal. However, she seemed to understand that she would have the help of the clan of men if she could slow it down for them to catch up. It was the way of her clan when hunting larger game. Mikolu envied her bravery.

When the bull turned sharply with lowered head to try and hook her with his horns, she let go of his tail, dived under his belly and nipped him on the knee of the opposite front leg. The attack forced him to turn again in the opposite direction, but when he did, she had ducked under him and grabbed his tail again.

By then, Waku had reached the bull. He plunged his spear deep in its side just behind the left front leg searching out its heart. Bellowing, the bull staggered and swung its horned head in Waku's direction. Waku dodged. Mika was suddenly there and drove his spear deep into the bull's neck to sever the jugular vein. Kifri still held the tail. The bull went down on its knees as Mikolu and the other hunters swarmed around it stabbing with their spears until it fell over on its side, kicked once and died.

In silence the hunters gathered around the bull their bloodied spears pointing skyward. The three oldest hunters, elders of the clan, spoke with Waku off to the side. When they joined the others around the bull, Mikolu knew it was time for his blooding.

Waku strode over to him, took him by the shoulders

and lead him to the bull. Then the chief of the clan put his hands in the blood from the bull's wounds and smeared it all over Mikolu's face, shoulders and chest. With a broad smile Waku said, "You have taken part in your first kill with the tools of manhood. I welcome you to hunt with us as long as the Great Kongai wills it so."

When Turu and Shonga drew their stone knives and made a move toward the bull to start the butchering of the meat, Waku held up his hand. "Wait, I am not yet finished." They stopped. Shonga glared. Waku turned back to Mikolu. "Mikolu, bring Kifri."

Mikolu picked up Kifri, who had been busy sniffing at the bull's nose as if she was not quite sure it was dead. She was quiet in Mikolu's arms though he felt her tense when he brought her to Waku. The chief again dipped his hands in the bull's blood. This time he rubbed it over Kifri's head, neck, shoulders and back. "Kifri is truly a gift from Kongai. She has braved Kur and helped us with a successful hunt. It is not wise to return such a gift. Kifri, Bush Thing of the B'sengi clan, you are welcomed to hunt with us as long as Kongai wills it so."

"Good, Kifri," Mikolu said as he put her back down on the ground.

She threw back her head and yodeled her victory call. Many of the hunters laughed and tried to imitate it causing more laughter. Mikolu squatted next to her and stroked her sticky coat as she sat back to lick herself clean of the blood.

Waku was smiling broadly, quite pleased. "Now let us prepare the meat. We have a long walk."

As Mika, Shonga and Turu began butchering the bull into smaller parts and the others bundled the meat in its hide for easier carrying, Kifri suddenly turned her cleaning attention to Mikolu. She put her front paws on his shoulders knocking him off balance. When he fell flat on

his back she licked his face, shoulders and chest with her
wet, soft tongue. It tickled and Mikolu tried hard not to
laugh.

Suddenly Waku was standing over them with a piece
of liver in his hand. "For Kifri," he said and dropped it to
her. Then, he left part of the rest of it and a length of intes-
tine on a nearby thorn bush as an offering to Kongai for a
successful hunt.

Kifri eagerly devoured her portion.

"I wonder, Mikolu," Waku said, letting his gaze wander out to the vast plains and distant herds. "Perhaps in
the season of birth if you could find a B'sengi den and
perhaps take a few pups."

Mikolu caught Shonga's fierce glance at the words, but
he did not care. Waku's words had awakened the joy in his
heart dispite having made an enemy among his own
people. The chief had seen what Kifri could do and wanted
more of her clan. On his word and the tales told by the
other hunters she would be accepted by the rest of the
clan now. "Great Waku," Mikolu said with pride. "If the
time comes when I can start a clan of B'sengi among us,
with the blessing of Kongai, I will."

CHAPTER 12

KUR RETURNS

Each hunter started the long walk back with as much meat as he could carry. There was meat for the feast and enough left over for each family to dry in the sun and pack in baskets for future needs.

Mikolu was given a place of honor at the head of the line for the long walk to camp. Kifri stayed at his side casting hungry looks at the haunch he carried strapped to his back.

He was tired by the time they reached the camp by the Sacred Baobab tree, but it was the pleasant kind of fatigue that always came at the end of a successful hunt. He turned the meat over to his mother, who immediately started cutting chunks from it for cooking.

While he waited for the feast, Mikolu cut up some meat for Kifri, who lay just beyond the smoldering fire pit. When he brought the meat to her, he found several of the hunters admiring her from a distance. They left when the scowling Shonga walked past towards his own fire, with hi s share of meat slung over his broad shoulders. "We will see how long she lasts among us," Shonga called loudly after the hunters and shook his spear at Kifri and Mikolu.

"You are angry because you are jealous that Kongai did not give you the gift of friendship with a Bush Thing of the B'sengi clan," Mikolu called back.

Shonga ignored Mikolu's words and kept on walking to his cookfire where Kufai, his wife and son, Luku, waited. Mikolu knew there would be trouble from Shonga in one form or another. He could feel the man's hate for Kifri as if it had become a living, unseen Spirit.

Mikolu fed Kifri and brought her water in one of his mother's wooden bowls. She joined him as he watched Kifri eat.

"You should not let Shonga bother you so," his mother said. "We must live together and there is no place for anger to grow into a feud."

"Shonga wishes Kifri dead or chased away, Mother," Mikolu said looking deep into her wise brown eyes. "He thinks she will bring Kur and others among the elders are taking sides with him, I know. I can see it on some of their faces."

"Kifri is new. They will get used to her and she will get used to them if Kongai so wills it and I believe he does. I was nervous about her myself, but she has proved she wishes to stay among us. From what I hear among the hunt-ers that passed my fire Kifri was a great aid in hunting today. There is much talk of how she stopped the wounded bull from running away by teasing it to stand and fight. Nendaka even says you are blessed with the gift of talking to Bush Things, which makes you very special." She smiled gently and went back to the fire to check the meat.

Soon all were gathered in a circle seated cross-legged on the ground. Wives and mothers brought cooked meat in woven grass baskets and seeds and roots in wooden bowls. Mikolu and Kifri were given a place of honor among the hunters next to Waku, who kept tossing bits of meat to Kifri.

When he caught Mikolu looking at him, he smiled broadly and said, "She is not such a wild Bush Thing now. I think perhaps we should find her a mate when the season comes, so that she may raise her puppies among our people."

It was something Mikolu had not thought of, yet. He smiled. It was a good idea. "Great Waku, I know just the clan of B'sengi to find. It is lead by a black dog and they hunt not far from here," Mikolu said as he took another piece of meat from the basket.

"Very good," Waku said, his smile growing broader. "It will be better than stealing pups from a den. We will do this thing when the season returns. We will take her to the land of the black dog and see that he finds her."

"And I wish to have one of her puppies," Turu, his friend, called from across the circle waving a rib at them. "After you have your choice, Great Waku."

Mikolu smiled at his friend and Waku laughed. Mikolu basked in the joyous moment like S'eech, the agama lizard on a sun-warmed rock. It felt good to be the center of attention after being away from all that was familiar. He knew life held few such moments and they were to be cherished.

When the food was gone and the darkness of night

stalked across the plains, Turu and a few of the hunters started the Pranga dance. To the clacking of dry T'woo bones and the rhythmic chant and stomping of feet the dancers jumped and moved about in a circle imitating the moves of Pranga to honor Kongai for a successful hunt and to celebrate a new pair of hunters in the clan. Mikolu was allowed to join for the first time now that he was considered a hunter.

Kifri watched with great interest, her head cocked one way then the other as she listened to the chant. When Mikolu passed her leaping like a Pranga, her curiosity and sense of play became too much for her. She trotted after him, jumping up and slapping his legs with her paws. He could hear the giggles of the women and young children at her antics. The laughter spread among the hunters and even those who still seemed unsure of her were caught up in the good humor of the moment. All that is, except Shonga who stalked away as soon as Kifri joined the dance.

Too soon the feast and celebration were over and everyone retired to their family cookfires. Each fire was fed with more branches to fuel them through the night so that no predator would enter the protective ring of light.

Content, Mikolu curled up by the fire not far from his mother and Mika. Kifri curled up next to him, her back against his back. She threw a lot of body heat and he kept pleasantly warm in the night chill between her and the fire. He was so tired that he dropped off to sleep almost immediately and dreamed of a litter of puppies scampering and playing in their camp.

The night was not yet over when Mikolu was awakened by hysterical screaming and shouting. Turu was suddenly at his fire, his face twisted with emotion, the whites of his eyes showing like those of a cornered Bush Thing. Behind him moving shadows between the fires became hunters carrying spears.

"Little Luku wandered out of camp and Kur took

him!" Turu shouted. "Shonga is going to kill Kifri!"

Mika and Shana were on their feet as several of the clan crowded about Shonga's fire across the way. Above the low voices he could hear Shonga yelling, "It is Mikolu's fault! The B'sengi has drawn in Kur and now my son is dead!"

Suddenly, Shonga pushed free of the people around his fire. He had his spear in his hand. He looked about. His angry eyes found Mikolu and Kifri by the fire and he threw his spear. Mikolu jumped up. Nendaka moved like lightning from the shadows. He threw his staff and struck down the spear before it reached Kifri. With a frightened squeal, Kifri scrambled out of the way of the falling spear and staff as they clattered to the earth.

Shonga started to run at Mikolu, but Waku grabbed him by the shoulders stopping him. There was a tense silence as the two men stared into each others eyes, a silence broken only by the sobs of Kufai and gentle, low talking of the women at his fire who tried to comfort her.

"I want that Bush Thing dead before it causes the death of all our children! Its scent has drawn Kur to our fires!" Shonga screamed out for all to hear.

Waku's wife, Bana, looked up from the sobbing Kufai. "It is not the fault of the B'sengi that your Luku wandered out of our camp. I was talking with her as she cut T'lak root and he was playing with Jeena's daughter. Who was tending them?"

"I demand my right to call the elders to council at first light to discuss the blood price for my son," Shonga shouted near hysteria. "Your nephew and that cursed Bush Thing for my son, Mika. I call for the banishment of them both from the clan!"

"You are wrong, Shonga," Mika said, walking forward, anger blazing in his eyes. "I am deeply sorry about Luku, but the B'sengi did not tell your child to wander. You have only yourself to blame. Luku could have been taken as easily by T'heea or Rowa. How do you know it was Kur?"

"It was Kur. I saw the tracks in the light of T'chuka's eye. The right front foot is missing a toe. And old Katuka saw him run off with Luku!" Shonga yelled, his voice cracking with emotion as he tried to pull out of Waku's grip.

"We will settle this in council in the morning. Nothing can be done now, Shonga. Luku is on his Soul Journey to the Creator Of All Things in the Hidden World and can not be called back even by Nendaka's most powerful magic," Waku said. "Kufai needs you now. Come."

Shonga let Waku take him back to his fire and crying wife. Mikolu felt his face go hot with fear and anger. Mika clenched both fists and returned to the fire. He looked from Mikolu to Kifri standing with her body pressed against his leg and her back hair up. His expression was one of deep concern that spread a dark frown across his broad features.

"Mikolu, this is bad. Very bad," Mika said and sighed deeply. "Kur likes to kill small Bush Things and our children. He has taken none of ours since he took your sister before you were born. But, now with Kifri in camp you can see why some blame her. I do not. But, Waku is right. Nothing can be done now. Try to get some sleep." Mika laid down heavily by the fire. Mikolu heard him sigh wearily.

Mikolu flopped down heavily next to Kifri. He stroked her head and back until she put her hair down. He watched Nendaka come to retrieve his staff and Shonga's spear.

"Try to sleep, Mikolu," the old shaman said. "It is the first test the bones have spoken of and the outcome is in the hands of Kongai. As I have said many times before, your path is different than the others and will be filled with many such hard tests. But, you are strong. Remember that,

Mikolu." The old shaman walked off into the night, a shadow within a shadow.

A deep ache settled in Mikolu's chest. He found little comfort in Nendaka's words. The shaman kept speaking of tests and a difficult path when all Mikolu wanted was to keep Kifri with the clan. He could not understand how such a simple thing could be so difficult. He feared Shonga would get his way. He was a powerful man with many friends. A Bush Thing among the clan of man was too new an idea for him and many others. With the death of a child no one would listen now. And worst of all, now that Kur had a taste for the flesh of man, he would return again. That fact alone put every clan member in danger, especially the women and children who harvested roots and dug grubs often wandering alone in the bush beyond the watchful eyes of the hunters. Kur could even grow bold from the ease of his first attack and come right into camp after more children. He might even catch Kifri off guard. Then, all would be lost.

There was only one thing Mikolu could do. He would hunt down Kur and kill him so he would never take another child. Mikolu knew he must make this hunt alone. It was a task he normally would not dare attempt without older hunters, but he had Kifri of keen scenting ability, speed of attack and courage. Besides, he was a man now and must settle his own blood feud with Kur who had not only taken Luku and put him in danger of banishment but had also taken his sister before he was born. Kifri, too, had something to prove.

He thought it best to leave long before the council of elders began the discussion of Shonga's blood price. Then, there would be no one to stop him on his quest. The thought of facing Kur chilled him to the bone. It was not from fear, but the kind of chill Nendaka had spoken of; nothing physical, but on a spirit level when a great truth had become known of an evil that must be defeated. A pool of dark magic was in Kur's heart and it was spreading to others. It was truly one of the tests the old shaman had seen in the bones. It was a test far more serious than missing the T'woo Mika had found or losing the Pranga to Rowa on the last hunt before his Long Walk. It was a test he and Kifri must not fail.

CHAPTER 13

TRACK OF THE CAT

The night insects were still singing in the bush and Eba, the eagle owl, called out of the distant darkness when Mikolu quietly walked past Mika and Shana asleep by the fire. His bow and quiver of arrows were slung over his shoulder. Silently he pulled the small net that would hold an egg shell from the bowls by Shana's feet. Kifri followed him on silent paws as he crept behind some bushes at the edge of the camp and looked out into the darkness to spot the camp guard.

Silhouetted against the setting night eye of T'chuka, Mikolu spotted Turu, leaning slightly on the shaft of his upright spear keeping watch. Turu was looking off in a different direction. Keeping thorn brush between them and Turu, Mikolu crept to where a long stick stuck in the ground marked the clan's dry season water cache of buried egg shells. Quickly, he dug one out and put it in the net sling hung on his belt. Then he left the sleeping camp followed by Kifri.

As Mikolu walked through a low patch of mist made silver by T'chuka's evening eye he looked one last time back at the camp. Nothing moved in the light of the fires. He could barely see one of the guard just beyond the furthest campfire. The guard was looking out at the open land and thorn brush in the opposite direction from him. The huge Baobab tree appeared as a ghost and in the shadows Turu was running silently toward him.

Mikolu quickly scooped up Kifri and ducked behind a thick thorn bush. In moments Turu reached the bush and stopped running. He looked at the ground and knelt to touch the dirt.

"Mikolu, I know you are here. Your tracks betray you," Turu said.

Chagrined at trying to fool his best friend, Mikolu put Kifri on the ground and stepped into the silvery light. "Why do you follow me?"

"Because you must not run away," Turu said. There was an urgency in his voice.

"I am not running away. We go to hunt down Kur and bring back his hide to prove he is dead. Then the blood price will be paid and the Elders will let Kifri stay with us."

Turu's eyes grew wide with disbelief. "You can't do this thing alone!"

"Sh-h-h-h-h-h! you will wake everyone," Mikolu admonished. "I am not alone. I have Kifri. She will warn me."

"She is but a mouthful for Kur. And you are two days worth of meat. Don't be foolish. Wait and tell the Elders you wish to hunt Kur and . . ." Turu started.

"She is too fast for Kur," Mikolu broke in. "And I am not fooled by his tricks of ambush. We are going to hunt him down and if you are my true friend you will tell no one where I have gone." He tried to search out Turu's eyes in the darkness.

Turu shook his head and shifted his gaze to the ground. He sighed deeply. Then, he poked a small stone with his toe and then looked back at Mikolu. Moonlight caught his eyes. There was fear and doubt in them. "I will not be able to live in peace with myself if Kur takes you. Please do not do this foolish thing."

"He will not take either of us," Mikolu returned adamantly. "Kifri will worry him like she did the young Oom bull. And I will shoot him with arrows. I have time to track him and catch him bloated with meat in the tree he has chosen to use as his larder. But, I must go now before he looks for water. Even then, I may catch him on open ground. Do not worry. Just keep silent." He turned away to leave unable to stand the pain in his friends eyes any longer.

"Wait!" Turu called after him.

Mikolu stopped and turned. Turu stepped toward him and threw his arms around him in a firm hug he instantly returned.

"Mikolu, you are like a little brother to me," Turu said in his ear. "I know this is something you must do alone. I will keep silent. I saw only Owa looking for scraps. May Kongai watch over you and Kifri and bless your hunt with success."

Turu released him and turned back toward camp not

looking back. Mikolu watched him a few moments and then headed deeper into the bush with Kifri.

Though it was still dark, Mikolu knew he could track Kur by both Kifri's keen sense of smell and the broken tips of dried grass and tracks in the dirt that he would be able to see in the pale light of the T'chuka's setting night eye. He hoped he would find the big cat by its food cache in the low branches of a tree where he would have a clear shot.

Mika had seen to it that he had plenty of practice with his own bow. Mikolu had no trouble hitting what he aimed at. Mika had started him with gourds as targets and had reduced the target size until he had him hitting small leaves stuck on acacia trunks with thorns. His first live targets had been large beetles, which he shot then ate. Now his target would be far bigger with the possibility of fighting back if cornered.

With the confidence of one on a sacred quest, Mikolu walked in a darkened world that waited for T'chuka's blazing day eye. He could just see Kifri's white tipped tail and legs ahead of him. "Find Kur, Kifri," he called after her as she ran back and forth, sniffing at the grass and bare earth. But, how would she know what he hunted?

When she paused to smell a bare patch of ground, he caught up to her. In the last of light of T'chuka's evening eye, he stared at the pale earth. There were two small dark stains in the dirt that seemed to have Kifri's attention. She sniffed and pawed at one. Mikolu knelt down and touched the stains. They were wet and sticky. When he touched his fingers to his lips he found his answer. Blood! He spat and searched the dry earth. There, he found the tracks of a big cat. A toe was missing from the right front foot. It was Kur. "Here, Kifri," he said. "Smell deep. It is this that we seek."

He walked a little way and stooped over, touching the tracks with his finger tips. They were as cold as the misty

night air. Kifri followed, poking her nose into them and
pushing his hand out of the way. She snorted and sneezed
at the dust she stirred up and looked up at him strangely
as if she was questioning the wisdom of hunting one of the
Kur clan. Then, suddenly she was trotting on ahead of him,
her head down on the scent line and her back hair erect.
He jogged after her, anger and fear knotting in his stomach
like two fighting S'heesh of the snake clan.

He had to jog faster through the tall, mist soaked grass
to keep up with Kifri. The scent trail was growing hot and
she grew more excited by the moment. As first red light
cut a bloody slash in the sky, Mikolu looked toward the
horizon and spotted a grove of acacia. Kur had to be there,
judging by the way Kifri was so intent on heading that way.

"Kifri!" he called after her not wanting her so far ahead
that she might be attacked. She stopped and looked over
her shoulder at him, her tongue lolling out of her mouth
and slanted eyes squinting at him. "Wait, Kifri."

When he got within half a bow shot of her, she turned
back to following the scent trail at a slower trot this time.
He slowed his pace and cautiously approached the trees,
his eyes searching the thorny branches for the least sign of
the spotted death. Kifri stopped a bow shot from the grove,
her hair still up and a growl rumbling in her throat.

The light breeze brought a scent in the air that gave
him a tremor of excitement. He waited there absolutely
still, sniffing the air and listening for the slightest sound. It
was the scent of an animal, a faint scent that came to him as
the slight wind changed and swung back again from the
acacia trees. It had the sharp ammoniacal smell of a cat,
not the clean almost herbal scent of a Pranga. In the largest tree to his right his eyes picked out something dark up
in the branches.

He pulled an arrow from the quiver slung over his
shoulder, notched it in the bow and pulled back ready to let

it fly. As he drew closer, he saw all too clearly what the dark shape was. In the jagged crook of a forked branch was crammed what was left of Shonga's son. The ribs showed white and glistened in the dawn light. The flesh of the lower half of his body was gone and eyes stared sightless from a small head that hung down on a neck that had been partly chewed to the bone.

Bile rose in Mikolu's throat and he gagged. He had seen death before when it took the old ones, but never one of his own clan half eaten by a Bush Thing. He forced his eyes away from the small body and back to Kifri. Once gain she was on the trail circling the base of the tree. Then, suddenly she was off again heading away from the tree and into the mist. Mikolu followed at a run.

Soon they reached the reeds at the edge of a large waterhole where a vast mixed herd of the M'un clan of wildebeasts and Rhaha were drinking and jockeying for position, sending dust up in a great cloud to mix with the morning mist. The grunts and moans of the M'un mixed with the barking challenges of Rhaha stallions in a confusion of noise that over powered the early morning songs of birds.

Mikolu eyed the reeds suspiciously. Kur could be hiding there on his way to get a drink after such a big meal. He was a master of stealth and the herds could easily miss him. When Kifri pressed her nose to some shorter grass before the reeds and then began casting back and forth with her hair raised down her back, Mikolu knew Kur was near.

Suddenly, a herd of the Ura clan, more than Mikolu could count on his fingers and toes, came out of the mist under a copper sky. One by one they appeared, as if the dark and massive stone-like animals with mighty curved tusks were not simply approaching, but were being created before his eyes. A young bull with a torn ear, full of his own growing size and strength broke from the others to charge right toward him across the shallow water flaring his ears, swinging his trunk and shaking his head in threat. Closer he came, his tree trunk-like legs curning the water to froth. To Mikolu, the Ura looked as if he would not stop.

Mikolu returned his arrow to his quiver and quickly looked about for cover. He saw Kifri break away from tracking and dash for a huge earthen mound built by the D'ika clan of termites that towered skyward like a red monolith worn away by time and rain. He followed her and saw her dive into a deserted Owa den in the base of the D'ika mound. The hole was big enough for him and he quickly crawled in bringing his bow with him.

There was hardly enough room for them to turn around and he had to crouch over to fit, but it was the only shelter that could stand up to members of the Ura clan, the outer wall being almost as hard as stone. When he looked out the den entrance, Mikolu saw Kur bolt from the reeds at the water's edge as the Ura bore down on him trumpeting a threat. So the big cat had been close by after all, Mikolu thought. Kur raced in bounding leaps for the forested side of a distant hill and towards the shelter of a pile of huge boulders. As, the young bull reached the D'ika mound, its massive, wrinkled legs blocked Mikolu's view and brought dust flooding into the den entrance.

More legs, like a forest of tree trunks, passed his narrow view out the den entrance and dangling trunks curled and uncurled. He and Kifri were surrounded. The elephants rumbled and trumpeted. Mikolu could hear the loud splashing as they entered the water to drink and bathe.

He and Kifri were trapped. All they could do was wait. The den was extremely cramped and bending over so long soon made Mikolu's back hurt. He shifted to a kneel, careful not to lean on and damage his bow. Kifri looked up at him her eyes wide and worried and ears back at an angle showing her annoyance with their situation.

Then, something hit the side of the D'ika mound hard and scraped along. Dirt showered down on them both. Mikolu saw tusks swing past, then poke the top of the den entrance. The tusks were pulled away and the D'ika mound was hit again. The deep, rumbling growl and trumpet blast of the young bull nearly deafened him and told him the Ura was practically on top of the old Owa den. Kifri jumped. He had to grab her around the chest to keep her from running out of their hiding place. She pressed herself tightly against him seeking security in his touch.

He saw the young bull back away from the den. It was the same young bull that had charged at him and scared Kur from the waterhole. Apparently he was practicing his fighting technique on their D'ika mound. Mikolu had often observed young bulls attacking everything from thorn bushes to D'ika mounds and even each other in their mock fights. But this time, he wished this young bull would pick another target.

Another deafening trumpet blast drowned out the sounds of the bathing elephants and the D'ika mound was hit once again. More dust rained down. Mikolu was beginning to wonder how much longer the mound could stand the punishment before the young bull found a weak spot and sent it crumbling around their ears.

Another Ura trumpeted behind the young bull. Mikolu saw the legs of the young bull pass in front of the entrance as he turned to face the challenger. He uttered a short trumpet and rumble and paced off after his rival.

Mikolu peeked out of the den entrance and spotted the two young bulls engaged in a shoving match, tusks crossed and trunks curled tight under their chins. A quick look left and right showed him he was still surrounded by the herd. There were several small calves with their mothers close to where he and Kifri were hiding. It was far too dangerous to leave yet. There was nothing more protective in the bush than a mother of the Ura clan. He had seen one kill one of three Rowa that had attacked her young calf when it had wandered just a little too far from her as she feasted on breadfruit. She had grabbed the big cat by a hind leg with her trunk and slammed it again and again against the trunk of an acacia tree until it was a bloody pulp while its two companions retreated and the calf hid behind her squealing.

No, he was not about to leave yet and provoke an attack. There was no way he could outrun an angry mother Ura or her companions who would defend the calf as if it was their own. He sighed deeply and backed further into the cramped Owa den to wait for the Ura clan to leave.

CHAPTER 14

CONFRONTATION

Slowly the sun climbed higher in the sky, burning off the mist. One by one the Ura filed from the water and the muddy edge of the waterhole. Brown and glistening from the mud, they picked up and slung the dry, red plains dust over their broad backs using their trunks. This was the sign for which Mikolu had waited for so long. They were truly finished with the days bath. The dust would cake on their muddy hides and provide protection against biting flies.

As the Ura clan moved off at a leisurely amble, Mikolu cautiously emerged from the Owa den on hands and knees with Kifri close behind him. Both were covered with dust. Kifri shook herself raising a small dust cloud and sneezed. Mikolu brushed the dust off his shoulders and out of his short hair. He checked his bow to make sure he had not damaged the sinew bowstring. Once he was satisfied all was in order, he headed toward the rocky hill where he had seen Kur retreat. They had lost valuable time trapped in the D'ika mound. The clan might miss him by now and trackers could be searching for him this very moment. He did not want them to find him until Kur lay dead with an arrow buried in his evil heart.

Kifri ran on ahead of him, bounding like a Pranga over large cushions of grass, pausing only now and then to sniff about searching. She slowed her mad dash when she hit the scent line again and continued to move at a slow trot.

By the time they reached the forested, rocky hill T'chuka's day eye was high and its heat raised shimmering mirages on the horizon and prickled Mikolu's skin. As he entered the welcomed patchy shade of the acacias, Mikolu paused to drink from the egg. "Kifri", he called. When she came to him, he stooped and poured out some water for her in his cupped hand. She lapped it up. He felt her tongue soft and gentle on his hand and poured out a little more water until she stopped licking. He replaced the grass stopper and squinted up at the massive jumble of rocks.

With great caution, Mikolu headed toward the rocks among the widely spaced acacia and fever trees. Kifri took up the scent trail again working the scent line that was now about her shoulder level having risen from the warm ground. She paused often to look back at him to make sure he was following. Her back hair went erect as she closed in on the rocks.

The jumble of huge boulders on the side of the hill

looked as if some giant hand had thrown them there, then scraped them together in a rough pile. Most were many times the size of an Ura and had created a maze of passages, some large enough to hide Shadur, the rhino. From exploring other such similar rock islands, Mikolu knew there would be many dead end passages where Kur might be hiding. He knew, too, that if he went into the rocks the big cat could easily trap him in one of these passages. He began to think that perhaps it would be wiser to climb a tree and wait for thirst to drive Kur back to the water across the open ground. Then, he would have an easy shot. Kifri changed his plan.

Kifri walked up a steep, wide dirt and pebble wash to the top of the first huge boulder that was partly buried in the hill. A young acacia with a twisted trunk had taken root between it and a more massive boulder behind and above it, pouring its dappled shade over both.

"Kifri," Mikolu whispered. "Kifri, come back," he called louder.

She did not look back at him. Instead she continued on and was quickly lost from sight behind the rocks. With grim determination, Mikolu followed her.

Once on the boulder, he glanced back over the shimmering plains. To his great distress among a moving herd of Pranga, he saw a lone hunter following his and Kifri's tracks in the mud by the waterhole. Distress quickly turned to panic as he recognized the hunter by his walk. It was Shonga.

An explosive snarl sounded above him. Heart skipping a beat, Mikolu's eyes instantly snapped to the source. Kur was crouching on the boulder above him, staring with those terrible green eyes that seemed to bore to his very soul.

Mikolu quickly notched an arrow and took a steady aim where the throat met the left shoulder. At this close range it would be a killing shot. Just as he let the arrow fly Kur turned away from him snarling and slapping at something behind him. The snarl instantly turned to a scream as the small, flint arrowhead imbedded itself in the muscle of the big cat's shoulder without hitting a vital spot. Kur leaped over Mikolu to another boulder and disappeared from view. Kifri suddenly appeared where Kur had been. A tuft of Kur's white tail tip fur was stuck in her whiskers.

"Kifri!" Mikolu shouted angrily. She had ruined the first clear shot he had ever had at the cursed Bush Thing. Kongai only knew if he would ever get another chance at such a good shot again. Now that the big cat was wounded, it would be more dangerous than ever.

Kifri ducked away from the boulder's edge out of his line of sight and Mikolu notched another arrow. Silent as a shadow, he stalked slowly around the boulder on which he had seen Kur land. "Oh, Great Kongai," he whispered. "Give me one more chance. Guide my arrow so that no more children will die in the jaws of Kur." He hoped he would have a clean shot before Shonga caught up to add more trouble to an already dangerous hunt. For Shonga to be tracking him alone, Mikolu thought, it must mean that Shonga intended only harm for him and Kifri. He had no idea where Kifri had gone in the rocks. He only knew that she would be after the big cat and prayed that she did not foolishly get too close.

Half way around the massive boulder, he found his way blocked by a steep jumble of smaller rocks from an old rock slide. They looked easy to climb, but he would need both hands free. He had no time to waste in finding a better way to the top. Reluctantly he took the arrow from his bow and returned it to his hide quiver. Then, slinging the bow over his shoulder, he scrambled up the rocks.

When his right hand grabbed a rock for balance just below the top, he heard claws tick on the rocky shelf above right below an overhanging boulder. He froze. Kur? It would only take one quick swipe of the big cat's paw to send him tumbling down the old rock slide from this precarious perch. He looked about frantically for a safer way up, ready to scramble down at the least hint it might be Kur.

Kifri suddenly appeared at the top staring at him from under the overhanging rock. He sighed deeply, relieved, yet he could not relax totally. Kur was close. He could almost feel the big cat's eyes on him.

Kifri quickly turned away rumbling a warning, her neck and back hair bristling. Expecting Kur to ambush him, he quickly scrambled to the ledge, unslung his bow and notched an arrow. At the far end of the boulder he now stood upon Kifri stopped to sniff at a broken arrow and drops of blood. By these signs Kur must have stopped to lick his wound. Though the spotted cat had chewed off the arrow shaft, the flint head had remained imbedded to torment him.

Suddenly, Kifri was scampering to the far edge of the boulder heading for more of the huge rocks that rose higher up the hill. She leaped across a narrow crevice to another huge boulder and headed toward what appeared to be a cave in the side of the hill. Mikolu followed easily leaping across the crevice as he rushed to catch up to her.

She stopped short a quarter of a bow shot from the entrance. She growled and dropped to her forequarters resting on her elbows her rump and tail up. Mikolu knew the gesture had a double meaning depending on the situation. It was a play bow or an indication game was close and Kifri was not playing.

As he crept slowly up behind her ready to let his arrow fly, an explosive snarl and hiss sounded from the blackness. Mikolu could not see a thing in the shadows, yet he knew the cave must be small and shallow perhaps with only enough room for Kur to hide. The snarl told him that this was not Kur's territory. The spotted cat had gone into the

cave out of desperation to escape and would attack if pressed
to the point it thought itself cornered.

Fear began to nibble the edges of his resolve. Doubt
settled cold on his shoulders like a morning mist. Perhaps
he was foolish after all to do this alone. If he did not kill or
seriously wound Kur with his next shot, Mikolu knew he
could very easily end up mauled or dead himself. He did
not like the idea of shooting blindly into the darkness. He
could miss all together or wound the cat and drive it out
of the cave to escape or attack. But, he had to do something. Shonga would soon catch up to him. He did not
know what Shonga's intentions were; to stop him from
hunting Kur, to kill Kifri, to kill Kur and further shame
him in the eyes of the clan? Yet, what ever his intentions,
they could not be good or Shonga would have brought
the other hunters.

Desperately, Mikolu prayed for a sign from Kongai as
to what to do. A small white stone half the size of his fist
and an arm's length away caught his eye. He shifted his
bow to one hand and picked up the stone. Kur rumbled
in the darkness. Mikolu could guess about where the cat
was from that sound, but he would be sure by baiting him
with a blow from the stone. He threw it hard, then took his
bow and arrow quickly in both hands and was ready in a
blink of an eye.

He heard the stone strike something soft. A snarl burst
forth and there was a flash of spotted gold and white in the
twilight darkness at the mouth of the cave. Mikolu let the
arrow fly. An eternity seemed to pass before a scream split
the darkness. A blur of spotted gold and white flew at him
from the blackness. The terrible green eyes were locked
on his. The jaws were half open. Paws bristling with claws
reached out at him.

Mikolu felt the front paws hit him hard. His breath
was knocked from him as the full weight of the cat followed

with the stinging pain of claws hooking into his chest The impact of the cat pushed him backwards. As he fell, he saw Kifri leap and grab Kur's tail. Mikolu hit the rock flat on his back his head striking the boulder. His world began to fade around him into a cold blackness he did not want to enter, but was powerless to stop. His last glimpse was of Kur turning away after Kifri.

Time and place were gone as Mikolu drifted helpless, unconscious. Then, sounds came to him, pulling him to semi-consciousness. Rasping snarls, yapping and the tick of claws on rocks. The snarls turned to coughing followed quickly by the light splatter of something wet on the rocks and then the soft thud of a large body. Pain in his head brought back the deeper darkness to blank out the rest.

A yelp tore into his unconscious mind and began to drag him back towards the real world again. He heard bare feet on the rock headed toward him. Shonga had found him.

"The Bush thing is dead," Shonga's voice reached him. "And they will find you, Mikolu, dead at the bottom of a cliff. I will tell the others that Kur sent you over the edge with a swipe of his paw. I will pull your arrow out of Kur and put one of mine in the wound so they will think I tried to save you and suspect nothing. The blood price will be paid and no more Bush Things will live among us."

He was aware of being picked up off the rock as Shonga 's voice slipped through the darkness again.

"Yes, you will soon join my little Luku. But unlike him, I hope you wander forever between the distant campfires in the sky as long as the mountains stand for bringing this grief to my family and the clan." Then Shonga screamed.

Mikolu's eyes opened to an upside-down, spinning world. They were almost at the edge of a cliff. He could see Kifri. There was a bloody gash on her right side. The B'sengi had her jaws clamped firmly just above Shonga's right ankle. Shonga suddenly dropped him and the blackness came again around the edges of his vision and he moaned aware his eyes were closing against his will. He wanted to fight back, but none of his limbs would work.

He heard the whoosh of air as Shonga swung his bow at Kifri and the ticking of her claws on the rock as she dodged the blow.

"I will kill you with my bare hands, Bush Thing!" Shonga yelled, keeping Mikolu from slipping farther into the darkness.

He heard Shonga scream again.

Mikolu was aware of bare feet and claws on the rocks again as Kifri dodged another blow. There was a sharp yelp when Shonga's third blow hit her. Then, Shonga grabbed him by the belt and began dragging him in the direction he knew was toward the cliff. He could hear Kifri nearby, growling a threat.

"Shonga, stop where you are!" came a shout. Mikolu knew the voice. It was Waku. Had Turu told him and the others of his plan to kill Kur?

"Put Mikolu down!" That voice belonged to Mika.

"Wait, Mika. Shonga it is over," Waku called again.

"I demand my blood price!" Shonga shouted.

"Kur is dead! The blood price has been paid! Put Mikolu down!" Mika yelled.

Shonga shook him with a strength that frightened Mikolu into opening his eyes to a blurry world. Shonga yelled, "He is the true cause of this. His life is my blood price! And the life of that cursed Bush Thing!"

Mikolu's vision cleared enough for him to see Shonga held his bow out like a stick in his free hand to fend off Kifri. He noticed, too that Shonga's leg was still bleeding from the deep bites Kifri had given him. She dodged every thrust of the bow snarling and snapping when it came too close. Her coat along her right side was stained with her own blood along a deep slash from Shonga's arrow, which had lodged in the thick muscle of her thigh. She had chewed off more than half the shaft. With the fierceness of a Rowa, she suddenly lunged and grabbed Shonga's bow in her teeth, snatching it right out of his grip.

The group of hunters used Shonga's momentary surprise at the dog to rush him. Mika grabbed Mikolu from Shonga.

"No! No! It is the law!" Shonga screamed in protest as Waku and several others pulled him down and pinned him to the rock only a few feet from the edge of the cliff. "I demand my blood price!"

Mika cradled Mikolu in his lap and rubbed some water over his face to wake him. Mikolu blinked his eyes and saw Waku leave the other hunters who held Shonga while he walked over to inspect the dead Kur.

The chief looked back at Shonga with cold, hard eyes. "You have tried to take the law into your own hands when none of us is permited by the laws of our Ancestors to do so. The Elders will now decide your fate, Shonga."

Mikolu tried to sit up. He noticed old Nendaka headed toward them across the rocks and then looked into Mika's eyes fully awake.

"Ah, he comes back to us," Mika said and smiled.

The pain from the deep scratches began to throb. Mikolu winced and said weakly, "Mika, Kifri. She drove Kur from me when he attacked." He looked down to find Kifri waiting patiently at his feet.

She gurgled at him and bounded up to his face to lick away the dripping water. He reached out one hand and ruffled her ears. Mika helped him sit up easing him down on the surface of the giant boulder as Nendaka reached them. Mikolu felt dizzy still and rubbed the back of his aching head.

Nendaka squatted down next to them both taking the

hide medicine bag from off his shoulder. Nendaka took a wrapped bowl of salve out and began to apply it to the claw marks. Mikolu winced at the biting sting.

"You have Kifri to thank for your life twice. Once for drawing Kur away and making the arrow do its work. And second for stopping Shonga from throwing you down a ravine." Nendaka quickly daubed some of the salve on Kifri's side wound while Mikolu kept her attention by ruffling her ears. By the time she yelped in surprise, the old Shaman was finished removing the arrow.

Mikolu was suddenly worried. "Where is Shonga?"

Mika pointed to Shonga, who was sitting on a pile of smaller rocks between two of the hunters. Shonga did not notice Mikolu's long stare. He sat with his shoulders slumped, staring at the rock beneath his feet as if it held something of secret importance. It was as if he was trapped in his own world of hate and could not speak.

"He does not seem so powerful and dangerous now," Mikolu observed. He felt Mika touch his shoulder.

"He only thought he had power because he could bully others with big talk. Grief has robbed him of all reason making him dangerous and he may strike out still. Turu saw Shonga leave our camp on your trail. He told Nendaka of his fear for your life and the promise he made not to tell of your hunt. When Nendaka told us, we knew you were in as great a danger as from the jaws of Kur," Mika said. "But the Elders will decide what to do with him."

Turu and Kuda, his older brother, came over carrying the limp, dead Kur between them with Waku leading the way. Strangely enough, Mikolu thought Kur did not look as big as when he was alive. His arrow was buried nearly to the feathers in the cat's left side and bloody foam still dripped from its mouth. They put it down and began to skin it with their stone knives.

"Shonga is too full of hate for you and Kifri, Mikolu,"

Waku said. "Such hatred has no place in our clan. I will advise the Elders that Shonga should be banished from us. He can go with his wife to live with her people by the river. It is a four day walk, but perhaps it will give him time to think about what he almost did to you and ask forgiveness from the Ones Above and the Ancestor Spirits."

Mikolu looked away from Shonga to the bloody carcass of the dreaded Kur. Turu and Kuda held up the beautiful spotted hide.

Nendaka put the wrapped salve bowl in his medicine bag and stood up. "The skin is yours if you wish to claim it."

Mikolu could not believe what he heard. He felt his mouth drop open. "But, I have no right to it. Only a Shaman can wear the skin of Kur's clan."

"Remember, Mikolu, I spoke many times of the different way you will travel. You are not like the others. The spirits call to you if you will but listen," Nendaka said with a stare that went to his very soul. Mikolu didn't understand.

Mika touched his shoulder. There was pride and a little mischief in his eyes. "You must have hit your head harder than I thought, Mikolu. Nendaka is going to take you and teach you his ways if you so choose and Kongai accepts you.

Mikolu looked at Nendaka. Nendaka gave him a wry smile. "Yes, you have truly proven you possess the magic of speaking with Bush Things and are blessed by Kongai. And, I will not live forever. Then who will cure the people and make hunting magic or speak with the Ancestor Spirits and the Unseen Ones?"

Mikolu smiled, but something nagged at him. "But, will I still be allowed to hunt and teach Kifri's clan to hunt with us?"

Nendaka looked at him with dark, serious eyes. "The way of the Shaman is a long, hard and often dangerous trail. You will be hunting for many years with the two clans before you give your life only to the Shaman's Way. The B'sengi clan will always be with you. Their friendship is your Gift to the clan. There is much to learn. But, you must first decide if this is the Life Trail you wish to follow. With the help of Kifri you must pass the last challenge the spirits will give. Think upon it, dance the Konga dance tonight with the other hunters. Enter the Dream Time with them as they dance and ask the Spirit World and Kifri for help. If they accept you in this final test, you will have the answer before T'chuka brings the dawn. Until then, Turu will prepare the hide of Kur under my instruction. You must not touch it until it has been purified or the evil in Kur's heart will take possession of your own and curse any magic you may make in the future." Nendaka took a small hide bag out of his medicine bag and poured some powder into a small bowl adding water from an egg shell. "Now, Mikolu, drink this. It will take away the pain in your wounds and head."

Mikolu obeyed and made a face at the bitterness. Mika and Nendaka laughed as he passed the bowl back. "If I become a Shaman, do I get to laugh at Mika when he must take bitter medicine?"

They all laughed at the question. Mika helped him to his feet and they began the long walk back to their camp.

CHAPTER 15

THE WAY OF THE SHAMAN

The Konga Dance had started at sunset and now T'chuka's night eye was high in a star decked sky. It was a dance of thanksgiving to Kongai for a successful hunt and a time to open oneself to messages from the spirit world. Each dancer wore a belt of the hide from Konga, the Eland clan, largest of all Pranga. Konga were sacred to Kongai and their meat only taken at the time of the equinox or solstice. Wearing a garland of vines around his head, Mikolu followed the other Konga Dancers shuffling around the fire to the hypnotic beat of chants and stamping feet of the clan Elders.

They danced long into the night. The faces in the fire-light around him began to blur. Mikolu became afraid as the world he knew began to fade. But, like the hunt for Kur, he knew he must pass this test. He would not fail Nendaka or his clan. He opened himself to whatever may come and cast into the darkness the question of his life path.

The Dancers became distorted with rainbow auras and wiggly lines as he went deeper into this new world. Some of the wiggly lines became a solid Bush Thing form. That form became Kifri running ahead of him. Chanting be-came an other-worldly murmur like a rain filled stream. Images flashed before him as the Dream Time came to bring things from the Hidden World.

Then far ahead of him, Mikolu saw Kifri chasing Pranga with others of her clan to a line of waiting hunters. Konga blurred out that image and Karaa, the hawk, flew past over this. The snarling face of Kur floated through and became the face of Shonga laughing hysterically, then shifted back to Kur. Then Kifri chased it all away.

The Konga images returned and changed from live Bush Things to their paintings on rocks in a place he had never seen. Then they shifted back to live Bush Things. A large Konga bull broke away from the others and headed toward him through the thorn brush. The Konga became a man with Konga hide wrapped around him and spiral Konga horns growing out of his head. The Kongaman smiled at him and beckoned him to follow with a fly switch made from an Konga's tail. "Come with me, Mikolu." His voice had the power of the raging rainy season storms. "Come with me and learn my secret ways. I am Kongai,

Lord of the Hunt and Bush Things. I have given you the gift
of friendship with the B'sengi clan in answer to your prayers.
Come with me, Mikolu. You have a special gift. There is so
much more to learn and share. Come with me." Kongai's face
grew to fill his vision.

Awestruck, Mikolu pulled away from the power. He
struggled with the fear and self-doubt in his heart. Then
he felt something touch his leg. He took his eyes off Kongai
a moment to look down. He found Kifri at his side. She
looked up at him. Her ears were up, her eyes bright and
her tail wagged slowly. She did not fear Kongai. Her very
presence gave him the confidence to go on.

"Come with me," Kongai's voice sounded again, but
this time it was a gentle as the bleat of a newborn Konga.

Mikolu looked back at Kongai.

He had changed again. His face was still that of a man.
Horns still sprouted from his head. But only the upper
part of his body was that of a man. Though he was still
draped in the Konga robe, Mikolu could see that the lower
part of his body was that of a Konga. He leaned on a staff
that was a twisted, live Baobab branch around which coiled
M'Sheea, the python. Eeak, the kingfisher bird perched
on his shoulder.

"Soon I must take back Nendaka to the Hidden
World," Kongai said gently. "Come to me, Mikolu. Let
Nendaka teach you. It is the secret yearning in your heart
that makes you so different from the others. Face it. Accept
it. Come to me." He held out his hand.

Mikolu reached out for it. When he clasped it in his
own it became the paw of Kur. He felt the claws in his hand.
Filled with terror he looked into Kongai's eyes. They became those of a Konga, soft and brown. Reflected in the
eyes were the stars and the full night eye of T'chuka. The
pain left and so did the fear. Then all faded.

Mikolu felt the earth come up and hit him. He only half

realized that he had fallen. He struggled back to conscious-
ness in a swimming motion as familiar voices drifted through
the darkness to him.

"Help him back, Mika. The first Dream Time is
difficult," Nendaka's voice broke through.

He felt his arms and legs being rubbed briskly as Mika
answered, "Yes, I know. I remember my first time."

Mikolu managed to sit up. He was dizzy. Turu was there
with a bowl of water. Nendaka took it and gave him a drink.
Kifri came to him out of the darkness to lick his face. He
hugged her, glad to be back in the world yet knowing she
had been with him all the while on the Dream Time journey. Then, Mikolu looked up at the questioning faces. His
eyes locked on Nendaka's.

"I saw many things . . . many frightening things and
Kongai spoke to me. He spoke of his gift to me of friendship with Kifri's clan. I saw the paintings of Konga on stone
in a place I have never been. I must follow your way,
Nendaka. I want to follow your way. I don't have to wait
until T'chuka returns to give you my answer. Teach me the
Secret Ways of Medicine and Magic. Kifri will be with me
always and more will come to join us. Kongai has shown
me all this."

Nendaka placed his hand on Mikolu's shoulder and
smiled. "When T'chuka's burning eye melts the night you
will begin your new journey. For now, return to Mika's fire
and sleep well. The journey tomorrow is long in many ways."

Nendaka turned away to help another dancer return
from the Dream Time trance. Mikolu heard the dancer
call out to the others," I saw the B'sengi clan hunting with
us. We will no longer lose game!"

He smiled glad another now voiced his vision to prove
the magic very strong. Then, Mikolu felt Mika's arm around
his shoulders and they walked to their cookfire with Kifri
following behind them.

Mikolu slept like the dead. The next day he, Nendaka and Kifri left the camp. Prepared to meet any challenge on the vast plains, Mikolu carried his spear and egg shell filled with water. Nendaka walked along silent with his walking stick and medicine bag slung over his shoulder.

They put a great distance between them and the camp through land Mikolu had not yet traveled. They passed a vast herd of Oom and Rhaha bathed in the pink light of dawn. Mikolu grew impatient. "How far are we going?" he finally asked.

"Not much further," came Nendaka's answer. "Be patient. We will go with Kifri to the Rock of the Bush Things you saw in Dream Time. It is a place where I and all the Shaman's before me have made powerful magic. It is there that we speak to the rocks by the images we make. It is how we make sacred pacts with Kongai and the Earth Spirits. It is where you must work your first magic that will mark your entry into my world between worlds by forever joining the clan of man with the clan of B'sengi.

Mikolu asked no more questions. When the midmorning sun began to prickle his skin with its heat, his answer took form. In the distant heat waves he saw a rock island. It was noon when they entered the welcomed shade of the grove of acacias at the foot of the huge boulders. He and Kifri followed Nendaka up a slanted boulder to a narrow trail between two towering boulders and ducked under the branches of an ancient fig tree. Here they squeezed their way through a crack in the rock to emerge into a sunlit, cave-like space open to the sky. The vertical rock walls were covered with paintings of Bush Things, people and swirling lines some layered over one another. Mikolu's eyes widened with awe.

"This is the place where dreams take form," Nendaka announced. "You were here in your Dream Time. It is a place of hunting magic and many wondrous things. Some

of these paintings were made by other wise shamans before I was born."

Mikolu walked up to one wall Kifri right at his side.
He stopped and placed his hand in a painted hand print.
When he looked farther up the wall he found the same
painting of the Kongai as he had seen in his Dream Time.
In awe, he blinked. They were still there. He felt Kifri's
paw on his leg and looked down. She sat at his feet. He
looked back at Nendaka and smiled. "This is all so beautiful. How is it done?"

Nendaka took his medicine bag off his shoulder and
placed it on the rock floor laying his staff next to it. Next,
he removed from the bag a bundle of Pranga hide tied
with a thong and brought it to Mikolu. There, he opened
the bundle revealing three small bowls holding a reddish-
brown, white and black pigment and several sticks chewed
at the end. "With these, Mikolu. These are tools of a very
special magic. A magic that starts within the heart," he said
and touched one hand to Mikolu's chest to emphasize his
words. "Here you shall have your first lesson in making
powerful magic. Watch and I will show you." The old Shaman moved closer to the wall. "First we honor Kongai by
committing his sacred animal to the Earth by painting it
on stone, the Child of Earth, for only the rocks and mountains live forever."

Mikolu looked on in awe as Nendaka deftly dipped
the chewed end of a stick into the reddish-brown pigment
and scrubbed it into the rock. A meaningless blob of paint
quickly became the head and shoulders and twisted horns
of a Konga. Nendaka then added some white on its face,
neck and chest bringing it alive. He finished by taking a
handful of dust and blowing it off his open palm at the
painting. "To the Earth I commit the image of Kongai in
thanksgiving for the gifts of life he bestows. May the Bush
Things be reborn and the rains forever come to bring back

the grasses." He then held out the stick to Mikolu. "Now it is time for you to bind the clans of B'sengi and Man together for all time by placing your image and that of Kifri on the rock."

Mikolu gingerly took the drawing stick and dipped it into the black pigment. He stared at the rock looking for a clear space to add his work. With a steady hand he drew an oblong circle above the image of an Oom. He looked at Nendaka unsure.

Nendaka smiled and nodded. "Let it flow from you, Mikolu. Magic will guide you."

Mikolu saw Kifri walk over to sit beside him. She looked at him curiously, then lay down next to him. He went back to work. The oblong became a head connected to a neck and then a body. Mikolu worked in legs and arms. In a rounded fist he put a short bow. It looked like a shadow with no features, but he felt it was him. Next he took the red-brown earth pigment. He started with another smaller oblong circle, then added a delicate pointed muzzle and pointed ears. He scrubbed the pigment into the rock and created a neck curved slightly down the way Kifri held her head when tracking. He added a body, slender legs and curled tail. When he was finished he looked again at Nendaka.

The old shaman smiled broadly at him. It made him feel proud and special.

Nendaka returned the pigments to his bag and took out a small gourd rattle. "Mikolu, do as I did. Blow dust at the images."

Mikolu obeyed as Nendaka shook the rattle past the rock picture a strange wailing song rising in his throat that sounded much like the call of the B'sengi. Kifri sat up alert and stared at Nendaka. The old shaman passed the rattle over Mikolu and Kifri. He chanted, "Here me Oh Kongai, Lord of the Hunt and Bush Things. Bind us with the B'sengi clan as long as the rains come, the mountains stand and the Earth gives birth to the stone."

Then Kifri, the dog that chose to live with men, pointed her nose to the sky and yodeled her strange call, "O-o-o-o-o-wa! O-o-o-o-o-w-a-a-a-a-r-r-o-o-o-o!" The gurgling howl echoed off the rocks and out to the plains announcing to all the world the dawn of a new age.

THE END